TITAN'S RETURN

TITAN'S RETURN

THE GREAT INSURRECTION™ BOOK SEVEN

DAVID BEERS

MICHAEL ANDERLE

DISRUPTIVE IMAGINATION

LMBPN Publishing
PMB 196, 2540 South Maryland Pkwy
Las Vegas, NV 89109

Version 1.00 December, 2021
eBook ISBN: 978-1-68500-430-9
Print ISBN: 978-1-68500-431-6

DEDICATION

For my brother, Danny.

— David

To Family, Friends and
Those Who Love
to Read.
May We All Enjoy Grace
to Live the Life We Are
Called.

— Michael

THE TITAN'S RETURN TEAM

Thanks to our Beta Readers

Kelly O'Donnell, John Ashmore

Thanks to our JIT Readers

Rachel Beckford
Dave Hicks
Jackey Hankard-Brodie
Diane L. Smith
Dorothy Lloyd
Angel LaVey

Editor

SkyHunter Editing Team

THE WRITTEN HISTORY OF THE GREAT INSURRECTION

As we flew into Phoenix's flames, we didn't know if we were going to win.

Sure, we were a lot better off than before Prometheus had begun his assault on the Commonwealth's fleet above, but even with the ground support, we were vastly outnumbered.

We were flying almost blind into a fiery world whose tunnels were filled with our enemy.

Every single one of us understood death was only a second away. All we needed to do was blink, and everything would be snatched from us.

Perhaps the only person who didn't know that was Prometheus since when the bloodlust was on him, he couldn't consider anything else. There was no possibility of death, of loss, only of conquering.

Even if his mind couldn't consider death, the gods could. For all Prometheus' greatness, he'd found himself in the greatest battle of his life.

He had finally met someone who matched his physical prowess, even if he refused to admit it.

CHAPTER ONE

Faitrin didn't need to be told anything, by anyone. She saw the blasts from Phoenix and understood immediately.

By the gods, he's doing it, was the only thought that went through her mind. With gray eyes, she took control of her fleet.

Fighter corvettes ripped forward into space.

Cruisers sprang closer to the Commonwealth's fleet and began firing the moment they were within range.

Jeeves spoke into her mind. *Thoreaux says he loves you.*

Faitrin said nothing in return, nor did she pause in her war commands. Thoreaux had left their dreadnought. He was leading his team into the tunnels that Prometheus walked.

He'll make it back, she told herself, so will Thoreaux.

Her job was to ensure that when he came back, everything in front of her had fallen into the flames beneath them. Her job was to kill Prometheus' enemies.

Thoreaux was in a teardrop-shaped attack ship with Caesar right behind him. The gigante faced the opposite way, his oversized hands doing their best to control the vessel's weapons.

Thoreaux was flying so damned fast, there wasn't a whole lot the giant could do, though.

A thousand teardrops flew with him, gifts from one of the warlords Prometheus had beaten; Thoreaux had known which when they'd received the bounty. Right now, he was simply hoping he could keep the thing from burning up when it reached the atmosphere. Then he would hope not to crash into the planet.

A lot of hope and not much skill.

These ships weren't meant to slow down. They were aerodynamically built to simply speed through space, but that was going to cause problems when they hit the fiery atmosphere.

Still, faster was better than slower when dreadnoughts were firing lasers along with corvettes and Pro's ship had made it through.

Thoreaux had hope and a huge gigante behind him, but not much else.

Faitrin was attacking the fleet.

Thoreaux was bringing reinforcements.

Relm felt the entire world shaking around him. The ceiling, the ground at his feet; all of it was rumbling.

The Terram in front of him looked frightened. Obs was still next to Monaham, doing as his master had said.

"Well, good sirs and madams, that's our sign. Up we go." He pointed his armored hand toward the panel, and despite the fear on the Terram's face, he darted to it. He scanned his hand and the circular door above slowly dropped, creating an opening into the cavern.

Relm didn't glance back. They had their orders.

He stepped beneath the hole, not bothering with the ladder, then bent his knees slightly and leaped through the opening.

Relm's MechPulse went to work.

CHAPTER TWO

Prometheus stood atop the table carved from rock. The bodies of those he'd vanquished lay strewn on the floor below him. None looked like the beast in front of him, though. Perhaps no human who'd ever existed looked like Hector de Gracilis, though Prometheus didn't care.

The room shook as if the gods themselves ran across the ground above. Prometheus still held control over much of the planet, his awesome mind waging war against the Commonwealth's fleet. He didn't yet know if help was coming, but as he stared at Gracilis, he cared little about that either.

At that moment, standing before a man almost twice his size, Prometheus only cared about killing. He would slay the one who had married his wife.

Gracilis' dual sabers were in his hands, lasers protruding from both ends. Pro saw that at least the bottom halves were capable of moving, though the tops seemed to remain rigid. Prometheus wore his MechSuit with the helmet retracted. He wanted the man he was about to kill to see his face. Pro's Whip hung at his side, then he started swirling it, first around his right shoulder, then his left. The lasers whirled at such a fast pace, the hum of air could be heard despite the room's rumbling.

He took two fast steps, crossing the distance between them faster than most humans could detect with their eyes. He swung low, going for the big man's knees.

Gracilis met Pro's Whip with his left saber, stopping it while the right slashed at his head. Prometheus barely avoided the swing, his hair singeing as he ducked toward the stone table. He swept his left leg and hit Gracilis.

The monster didn't flinch as the metal MechSuit smashed into his shin.

Pro saw the saber swinging toward his chest milliseconds before contact and shoved himself backward with his right leg. The saber burned through the top layer of metal on his chest but went no deeper as he skidded across the rock table. Gracilis leaped toward him, both sabers at the ready. Pro came to a stop and rolled, barely missing the beast's armored knee. Gracilis hit the rock table, and the right edge broke off. Dust filtered into the air.

Pro came to his feet, but the beast was moving as well. Given his size, he shouldn't have been able to move that fast, yet he was almost on top of Prometheus again.

Gracilis' sabers collided with the red Whip as both slashed forward, trying to gain ground. Prometheus found himself giving way, unable to keep up with the beast's dual-bladed speed. The room was shaking harder, and dust was falling from the ceiling. He could stop the attack on the fleet or fight harder here, but then his followers would be doomed.

He had to do both.

Pro was getting closer to a corner, and at this point, he was just doing everything in his power to keep the sabers from taking off a limb. He saw the light-blue Titan in his peripheral vision. She remained against the wall, her Whip in her hand with the lasers furled. Pro would have no chance if she entered the battle.

He felt the corner coming up quickly. If he ended up there, he was dead.

Just before reaching it, Prometheus spun, his feet like a dancer's and his Whip a blaze of light. It was the first time he'd moved faster than the monster, and he found himself out of the corner with Gracilis backed into it.

Nothing fazed the creature, though. Just because his body had been outmaneuvered didn't mean his mind had. His face showed no shock, and his massive leg rose into the air. He kicked with a speed that defied physics.

Pro could do nothing to stop it.

He rose into the air. His suit had taken the brunt of the attack, but his mind knew what was coming from behind. His helmet started rolling out and had barely covered the back of his skull when he hit the rock wall. Pieces broke and crumbled and dust sprang up around his frame. Behind him was an imprint of his body.

Pro's Whip dropped slightly but not out of his hand. His helmet finished wrapping around his skull as he looked up.

The beast was charging him, sabers ready to finish the job. Prometheus had perhaps not even a second before he'd be impaled. He dropped and, using the wall as his brace, launched forward. He hit Gracilis' legs with his left shoulder, unable to maneuver his Whip to cut the man. The beast rose into the air, and Prometheus continued flying in the opposite direction.

Using his left hand, Pro touched the ground and flipped back up on his feet.

Gracilis had hit the wall headfirst and was turning around slowly, dazed by the impact with the rock. He was turning while trying to regain his feet, but the right one slipped out from under him. He fell on his back, and Pro saw his opening.

To his right, something fell from the ceiling. The room, and perhaps the entirety of the world, was falling apart. Prometheus ignored it. He rushed forward and leaped, ready to finish this. His right hand held his Whip. The three strands were wrapped into a pointed blade as he came down on Gracilis, but even when dazed, the man's power was incredible.

He'd been holding both sabers but dropped the left one when he saw the former Titan coming. As Prometheus came toward him, Gracilis reached his long left arm up and grabbed Pro's right wrist, forcing the Whip away from its intended target.

The laser cut through the very top of Gracilis' shoulder and continued into the stone beneath.

Simultaneously the Martian's right hand thrust his saber up, finding Pro's shoulder and shoving it deep.

Pain exploded across his torso. Inside his helmet, his teeth clamped together, and he shoved down a scream.

Gracilis didn't slow. He started to pull the saber down, moving the laser toward Pro's heart. If he got there, it was all over.

Pro knew the grip on his wrist was too strong, his Whip too deep in the stone. He couldn't pull it free from this position. The pain in his chest was growing, the laser cutting through metal, bone, tendon, and muscle.

If he didn't do something now, he was dead.

Prometheus reared his head back and slammed it into Gracilis' face.

The Martian's nose broke, and blood spurted across his face. Still, he continued to drag the laser, millimeter by millimeter, closer to Pro's heart.

Enraged, in pain, and nearly mad, Prometheus reared his head back again and slammed it down.

Again.

Again.

Finally, the laser stopped moving, and Gracilis' broken face fell back. His right hand slipped from the saber, and his body went slack. His nose was a wrecked thing, swollen and blue. His orbital bone had been fractured, and his eye was beginning to close.

Prometheus dropped his Whip, thinking only of removing the saber still burning in his shoulder. With his right hand, he grabbed the hilt and pulled. The weapon slowly slid from his body, and he flung it across the room as if it were a poisonous snake.

Pro slumped and then fell on his side. The two warriors lay shoulder to shoulder.

The room had stopped shaking. Prometheus had lost control of the planet. Lying next to the giant, he struggled to remain conscious. The pain was too great, and his mind could hardly handle it.

The light-blue Titan had stepped into his field of vision.

Her Whip was unfurled now, and she appeared to be staring at Gracilis. She said nothing, though.

Prometheus knew what she was doing: calling for backup through her MechSuit's comm. She was trying to figure out what in Hades was going on beyond this room as well.

I'm not done, Prometheus thought. Blackness was encroaching on the edges of his vision. He took a deep breath, focusing his mind, and the darkness slowly receded.

He could feel his Whip. It lay on the other side of Gracilis, waiting for its master to command it.

With his mind, Prometheus reached for it, and the hilt rose into the air, finding his right hand.

It didn't even have time to unfurl. The light-blue Titan's armored foot kicked Pro's hand, sending the Whip clattering across the room. His head flashed to the right, following it with his eyes. From the corner of his eye, he saw the blue lasers twirling around his left shoulder, ready to finish the saber's job.

He couldn't retrieve the Whip, not before she killed him.

Alistair stepped forward, Prometheus heading behind the mental door again. Using his legs and right hand, he pushed himself back against the wall. Gracilis was still out, though his face was twitching as if he were regaining consciousness.

Alistair turned his helmet to the Titan. Her callsign was Aletheia. "What do you want to do from here?"

She didn't bother with him but stepped across the room and picked up the discarded Whip. She hooked it on her belt, her own Whip still alive at her side, then turned to the closed door.

Alistair didn't need a Commonwealth comm to understand what was happening outside. His plan had somehow worked and the battle was once again flooding the planet's tunnels. Now Aletheia was stuck here with an injured leader and an injured enemy, unsure of where to go or how to get there.

Alistair's pain wasn't any less, but he wasn't on the verge of passing out anymore. He looked at Gracilis once more. The man's face had been obliterated; he'd need surgery. Alistair knew the two of them weren't finished. Alistair couldn't kill him now, but he would, or at the least, he'd try.

"What are they saying over your comm?" Alistair asked without looking at her. He wanted to regain his feet, but he wasn't sure how badly it would hurt. He needed his wits right now, and a black cloud taking over his vision wouldn't help with that. "We don't have to die in here," he told the Titan. "You just need to let me know what they're saying."

"What about your comm?"

Alistair shook his head and decided he didn't want to be between the Titan and the Martian when he finally awoke. Using his right hand, he slowly guided himself up the wall until he was standing. He was forced to lean over, placing his right hand on his knees, and take a few deep breaths.

"It's broken," he told her. "When he kicked me into the wall. What are you hearing?"

"Quiet, Subversive," she shot back. "You and I aren't a

team. You're my prisoner. I might have orders to keep you alive, but that doesn't mean I'll follow them."

A loud boom came from somewhere beyond their door. Alistair smiled inside his helmet. His people were fighting, and it was a good sign to hear that explosion. It meant they'd breached the tunnels.

It meant the insurrection still had a chance.

Alistair straightened as the feeling that he might pass out faded. He moved to the other side of the room. Gracilis was coming to, beginning to blink. Pro watched as Aletheia knelt beside him. She still held her Whip, though the strands had partially retreated into the hilt.

Alistair's mind seized his Whip, which was still attached to her belt. Aletheia's hand dropped to grab it, but she was too slow. It flew across the room into Alistair's palm. His fingers wrapped around it, and the red lasers spilled out.

He didn't move. Physically, he couldn't do anything right now, and he knew it.

Gracilis pushed himself up, his broken face grimacing.

Aletheia handed him one of his sabers. He'd grabbed the other as he got off the floor.

Alistair's mind reached beyond this room even as his eyes monitored the people inside it. He needed to know what was happening elsewhere, but he couldn't spend much time outside this area, not with this injury.

Thoreaux was here. Servia, too. Caesar was in the tunnels somewhere, as was Nero. He couldn't reach Relm, but he knew Obs was still alive. Their connection spanned more than worlds.

We might win, he thought. *We might win this.*

Alistair wasn't dying right now because the laser had

cauterized his flesh. He was injured but not bleeding to death. It wouldn't last forever, though. He needed medical attention fast.

Gracilis was staring at Alistair. He held his sabers in his hands. His face was grotesque, and Alistair knew the man's blood was on his helmet.

"Situation report," the Martian said into his comm.

A few seconds passed with Alistair standing on the other side of the room, holding his Whip. It sounded like the explosions were getting closer. Alistair didn't use his mind to venture out again. He didn't have the physical strength to divide himself, not if Gracilis wanted to fight.

After those few moments, Gracilis met Alistair's eyes. "I won't fight you with that injury. I won't have it steal my glory. You're coming with us, so drop the weapon."

Aletheia stepped closer to Alistair, her Whip twirling at her side.

Fighting now would be futile. Alistair killed his Whip, then tossed it to her. Aletheia caught it easily before looking at Gracilis.

The Martian's eyes remained on Alistair. "We're taking him to the portal, then getting off this planet and back into Commonwealth territory."

He didn't need to say the rest, but Alistair knew. Inside his helmet, despite the almost crippling pain, he smiled.

They were losing the planet.

The insurrection was taking it.

The armor on Relm's left leg was damaged. His knee plate wasn't working properly, and his knee hurt like Hades. His arms still worked fine, though, and using his MechPulse, he was scattering the living as if they were dolls.

The cavern had been emptied about ten minutes prior. One of Aspen's banshees had taken a mortal shot, and she remained where she'd fallen. It wasn't something any of them wanted to do, but they had to take the planet if there was any hope of giving the woman a proper send-off.

The other two banshees and Relm had cleared the cavern, then one of them rushed off with Aspen and Obs, hopefully heading to a weapons cache.

Relm limped his way through the cavern toward the trap door on the other side. The banshee—he couldn't remember her name to save his life at the moment—was watching his six. Relm's arms were tired, but he kept his pulse at the ready.

Many of the enemy had fled when the attack came. Relm didn't think it was out of fear; he believed they had been commanded to get their asses somewhere else. Pro had done a number on the fleet from what Relm had heard over his comm. Thoreaux's and Servia's crews had made landfall too.

Relm reached the door leading into the hidden tunnels. He paused as he spoke into his comm. "Monaham, what's it look like on your side?"

In the ensuing moment of silence, Relm's heart jumped into his throat. Monaham was dead. That was why he wasn't answering. This was all over.

"Weapons secured. Half the team is fighting on this side

of the planet. The rest of us are heading to secure the trains."

Relm took a deep breath, relief shoving his heart back into his chest. "You're going with them?"

"Roger," came the response, with no explanation.

That was shocking. The man was terrified inside these tunnels, but he was heading back into the fight even after having accomplished his directive. Pro was a scary judge of talent if nothing else.

"Is Obs okay?" Relm asked.

"Physically, yes. Something's wrong with him, though. He's still at my side, but he's whining a lot. I don't know what it is."

Relm did. "Look, just take care of him. If he falls or looks like he's severely hurt without any physical injuries, you get right back on this comm with me immediately. Got it?"

"Roger."

"Okay," Relm said. "I'm going to try and find Pro. You keep going to the trains."

The connection was broken, and Relm found himself staring at the hole in front of him.

"What's the plan?" the banshee asked from behind.

Relm didn't answer. His thoughts were on Obs and what his distress meant. If the animal was acting strange or hurt, something wasn't right with Prometheus. "Give me a moment," he responded to the banshee, then said into the comm, "Does anyone have eyes on Pro?"

Thoreaux was the first to come back. "No."

Servia and Caesar were next. "Nothing."

"We've got a problem," Relm said. "Obs isn't acting

right. Something is going on with Pro. We need to find him."

Faitrin spoke from her perch above the atmosphere. "The ground attacks have ceased. I don't know what that means. We're in decent shape up here right now, but there's no more support from the planet."

Thoreaux's voice came over the comm again. "Obs is alive?"

"Yeah, he is," Relm said. "But he's acting like he's hurt."

"Caesar," Thoreaux spoke again, "you're the closest to the portal. How long will it take you to get to it?"

A few seconds of silence as the gigante checked.

"Twenty minutes."

"Get your crew over there," Thoreaux commanded. His voice brooked no discussion. "Servia, continue as you were. Relm, you do the same. I'm taking my group to the portal too, but we'll be a little bit behind you, Caesar. Everyone on board?"

"Got it, broth," Relm responded.

"On my way," Caesar confirmed.

"Understood," Servia finished.

The conversation ended, and Relm looked over his shoulder at the banshee. "Time to go help your boss."

I hope mine remains alive, he thought but didn't say.

Relm dropped down the black hole while others on the planet raced to find their leader.

Caesar turned his group of gigantes. He understood why Thoreaux was pointing him toward the portal. If

Prometheus was still alive, and he had to be because Obs still lived, he was in trouble, and the Commonwealth was trying to steal him. They were going to get him off this planet and into the cold embrace of their galaxy.

Everyone in the conversation knew it, so there wasn't any need to ask.

Caesar had to stop it from happening—he and his brothers.

The gigante saw nothing as he went forward. He simply killed those who got in his way, knowing his duty right now was as important as it'd ever been.

Those behind him killed just as mercilessly, leaving bodies and screams in their wake.

He'd told Thoreaux it'd take twenty minutes, but Caesar got there in twelve.

The cavern was massive, larger than any underground room he'd ever seen. It had to be, though, given what it housed. Caesar had never seen one of these gates to other galaxies, but he'd heard about them.

He wasn't sure any of the gigante traveling with him had seen one either.

The group stopped at the lip of the cavern and stared down. An arch stretched from one side to the other, its top nearly scraping the rock ceiling. Caesar didn't understand the engineering necessary to create such a room or build such an arch inside it, but he couldn't help but marvel at the accomplishment.

The arch glowed, deep blue light shining from whatever material created it. Huge white lights shone from the ceiling, carved into the rock, illuminating the craggy floor beneath.

"Thoreaux," Caesar said into his comm, "we are here. I do not see Pro. Could he already have gone through?"

Thoreaux's response was immediate. "Give me a second."

Speaking in the gigantes' language, he instructed his team to step back from their high spot. There were multiple entrances into this place, some on the ground level. Caesar didn't want to be spotted, at least not immediately.

"Caesar, you there?" Thoreaux asked.

"Here."

"Obs is still acting weird, but he's not freaking out. I think if Prometheus was off-planet, the animal wouldn't know what to do with himself. Stay there. I'm on my way."

"Understood," the giant said.

The comm went silent, and without speaking, Caesar pointed at his team.

No one said a word, but they spread through the cavern, ready to take back the fire-bringer.

***

Thoreaux's question still rang in Aspen's head.

What's Obs doing right now?

Aspen de Monaham, brother of the great Ice Queen, was staring at the drathe. He'd been leading a contingent of scared men and women, but they'd taken five of the trains and were now heading toward the main population points to meet with the rest of the insurrection forces.

Aspen hadn't known he could do any of what he'd just

done, and at some point in the future, he'd have to consider it.

Right now, though, he couldn't think of anything but the drathe. The animal was shivering at his side as if he were cold or going into shock. Aspen had touched the creature's fur and he felt warm enough, so it had to be something else.

The whining was different from any animal Aspen had ever heard. It was constant, and though Obs didn't move from the man's side, it was obvious he wanted to. Whatever control the animal possessed, he was using all of it to remain seated.

"What is it?" Aspen asked from his spot on the train. The car was crowded, with short, muscular Terram surrounding him. Each held a weapon, some more than one. Many had injuries, but all were ready to kill if necessary.

Obs didn't appear to see anything on the train. He stood on all fours, his back higher than Aspen's waist. It wasn't until the man spoke that Obs looked up at him, turning his head slightly to the left.

"Is it him? Prometheus?"

Obs stopped shivering at that and turned around, bumping some of the Terram out of the way as he did. Guttural curses could be heard, but Obs didn't care. He stared up into Aspen's eyes.

"You want to go to him?"

The drathe let out the loudest whine yet, sounding as if his heart was breaking.

Aspen looked to his left, checking the panel's destination points. "You think you can get to him, Obs?"

The animal responded with a deep growl. That message was as clear as the last: he'd get to his master no matter what got in his way.

Aspen looked at the Terram they'd met in the tunnel. He'd been helping Aspen since they'd started their murder march. "Slow the train and let the animal off at the next depot."

The Terram didn't question the order, just nodded and touched a few places on the panel floating in front of him. The train started slowing, and within three minutes, it'd come to a stop.

Obs leaned forward and nuzzled Aspen's hand.

The leader of the de Monaham family squatted so they were at eye level. "You did your duty here. Go find your master."

The animal turned as the Terram moved out of his way. The train's doors opened and Obs bounded off, hanging a quick left, then leaving Aspen's line of sight.

He didn't know how Obs would find Prometheus, but he understood Pro needed the animal more than he did.

Good luck, Obs. Bring him back to us.

Three people understood Alistair's injury: him and the two from the Commonwealth.

Outside of them, only Obs understood that his master was hurt. Badly, too.

Obs felt as if something were ripping apart his shoulder, though there wasn't any visible injury.

The animal couldn't tell time like humans, but he

understood his master had been hurting for a while and that the pain was growing worse. Obs was weakening at the same rate as Alistair, and the drathe knew they were moving his master. They were taking him somewhere, and it wasn't any of their friends directing him.

That was what the animal knew. That was all he needed to know.

It was more than enough. His master needed him.

Obs ran through the halls, looking like the wolf that guarded Hades. Three times he came upon enemy soldiers, and he pounced and ripped their throats out before they understood what was happening. Each attack took even more out of the animal, weakening him.

He had to conserve energy. Alistair would need it soon.

The animal went on, heading toward a cavern he didn't know existed, using his master's bond to direct him.

CHAPTER THREE

It was getting harder to walk. With each step Alistair took, it felt like the blade was carving into him again, like it was still burning him. He'd pushed back his helmet since the air conditioning vents in it had been damaged and sweat was pouring down his face.

They reached another elevator, and Alistair blindly stepped on. He found the nearest wall and leaned against it.

Aletheia and Gracilis didn't need any support. The giant's face might have been damaged beyond recognition, but it didn't appear to be affecting him. The Titan was in fine shape, having not had to battle anyone.

The only person suffering in this elevator was Alistair, and he knew he needed medical attention soon. He was no doctor, nor had he any idea what was going on inside him from a detailed perspective, but he understood he was weakening. Fast.

The elevator stopped, and the doors opened. Alistair looked out at a cavern that stretched as far as he could see. He remembered the first portal he'd seen back on Pluto when Lync had shown it to him. He remembered how mesmerized he'd been that it existed.

Another one was in front of him now, but he felt no awe. Alistair didn't even know if he was going to make it across the cavern to be transported to another galaxy. He could very well die a quarter of the way there.

Gracilis stepped off first, Aletheia following. The Martian turned to look at Alistair's slumped figure, still leaning against the elevator wall.

Alistair wouldn't beg these people, nor would he be dragged across the rock cavern.

He slowly straightened, dark spots dancing across his vision from the pain. His teeth clenched, but he stepped off the elevator.

Gracilis spoke. "Are you going to make it?"

Alistair's eyes found the mutant's. "I'll make it."

He didn't have to search far or hard to know Caesar's gigantes had surrounded the upper level of the cavern. He felt Obs too. The drathe had abandoned his duty of remaining next to Aspen and was rushing toward him.

Help was on the way.

Alistair just had to remain standing.

Caesar watched his leader step out of the elevator. It'd come from beneath the cavern, and there appeared to be only two Commonwealth guards. One of them was the largest human Caesar had ever seen. From this viewpoint, he couldn't judge him against a gigante; he only knew the man dwarfed Prometheus.

The other was a Titan, and Caesar had dispensed with many of them already.

"On my signal," he whispered into his comm. "Thoreaux, I see Prometheus. Do I have your permission to intercept? He appears to be severely injured."

From where Caesar stood, he could see Pro limping. It worsened with each step, and Caesar thought without that MechSuit supporting him, he'd have fallen to the ground already. Pro wasn't doing well, the giant was sure of that.

Thoreaux's voice came back through the comm. "Don't let him go into that portal, Caesar."

The gigante nodded. To anyone looking at him, he appeared calm and measured, but inside him, rage was growing.

The man beneath had saved him from a life of slavery.

He'd saved all of Caesar's brothers, risking his life to do so.

Now, the Commonwealth was trying to take Prometheus. They were trying to steal the man who had brought life to so many.

"On me," he whispered into the comm.

"3...2...1."

Alistair saw Gracilis stop milliseconds after the gigantes showed themselves.

They used GravityFeet to leap over the railing. Fifty of them floated out of the sky like giant gods, and Alistair wasn't sure he'd ever been happier in his life.

Gracilis' sabers were alive in his hands at once, as was Aletheia's Whip.

The giant mutant was behind Alistair in a few steps, his saber across the man's throat and his hands pinned behind.

The gigantes stopped their forward movement.

Caesar stood about fifteen meters away, holding his sabers. The tiny insects from his and the rest of his kind's hands were floating out into the cavern. Caesar understood that Alistair was injured. The insects slowly moved toward him, though he felt Gracilis' massive hand tighten on his. He didn't understand what they were.

"Stay where you are," the Martian demanded.

Caesar took another step forward. Alistair saw the first insects land on his MechSuit, the biotech creatures knowing where the wound was.

"You're not going through the portal," Caesar said in his stilted Solarian. Now that he was closer, he thought Gracilis might be slightly larger than him. The man was unbelievably big. "Not with him, at least." Caesar pointed a saber at Alistair.

Aletheia stepped to the far right, creating space between the two warriors. Alistair knew it was a smart move as the beginning gambit: split the gigantes up and cut them down before pulling together.

More insects reached Alistair, and a thick cloud was growing overhead.

Alistair felt Gracilis' hand tighten and knew a decision had been made. Later, he'd understand that this decision was the Martian's. He'd sooner die than retreat.

Gracilis pushed Alistair toward the portal, then kicked him *hard* in the back. Almost helpless, Alistair rose into the air, pain blanking out every other thought in his mind. He rushed toward the portal, the hum of the technological marvel vibrating his bones.

He felt the thing pull him closer, the underlying science of the black hole that made such things possible reaching out for him.

Alistair hit the ground and tumbled forward, the pull on him growing. His right hand grabbed protrusions in the rocky floor, halting his movement toward the portal. He was about two meters from it.

Alistair looked up. The insect swarm had followed him, but he didn't know if it'd be too late. His vision was darkening again.

Figures moved before him, but he was losing his ability to differentiate friend from foe. Lasers and plasma spilled across the cavern. Finally, Alistair couldn't hold his head up any longer. It fell to the rock beneath him.

The portal continued pulling his body closer one centimeter at a time.

Caesar saw the giant man kick his leader across the room as if he were a child. Prometheus rose into the air as if he weighed nothing, then fell to the ground. Caesar saw his strength and the first thought which came to him was he had to serve this man. Whoever this giant creature was, he was the strongest person Caesar had ever come in contact with.

No, he told himself. *Prometheus set you free. You don't serve strength. You serve leadership.*

His eyes moved away from his fallen leader to the man who had felled him.

The unnamed giant was moving toward Caesar faster than he'd ever seen anyone move before. His two sabers had lasers at both ends, which would pose a problem.

He backed up quickly, using his sabers to knock away the man's attacks. He saw in his peripheral vision that the Titan was on the move, yet she should have been easily overwhelmed by the gigantes.

That hadn't happened.

The Commonwealth's backup had arrived, and they were streaming through the multiple entrances. Caesar had shown up with fifty gigantes, but they were quickly outnumbered.

He had no time to consider it. The man-beast was upon him.

His sabers were a blur of color, lasers darting left and right, up and down. Caesar was doing everything in his power to keep from being slit open, but he understood, as Prometheus had earlier, that he couldn't keep up with this creature.

The insects had quit flowing from his palms. He needed all of his focus on this man if he was to survive.

Caesar kept retreating, seeing more and more of the Commonwealth arriving. His group was outnumbered, and in the distance, Caesar saw Pro lying unconscious on the ground.

A saber sliced through Caesar's thigh, opening it wide. He didn't glance down, knowing that to do so would end his life, but used his other leg to launch himself back.

He put two meters between him and the whirlwind, but

that was next to nothing given how fast the man moved. Caesar spoke into his comm. "Thoreaux, we have lost. We cannot get to Prometheus."

Thoreaux's voice whispered back through the comm, "Don't move."

The man-beast had reached him. Caesar raised his blades to stop the attack while understanding death was upon him.

The first pulse blast nailed the man-beast's left arm. It disintegrated his armor and burned into the flesh beneath.

The saber from his right hand swung at Caesar's head, and all the gigante could do was fall backward and hope he survived.

The second pulse shot savaged the attacker's arm, then Thoreaux hit the ground next to where Caesar lay.

The gigante tried to get to his feet while skittering back to gain distance from the warrior. The giant man showed no pain despite his left arm having been rendered useless. Caesar could see muscle and bone that skin had covered moments before.

Still, the giant turned his attention to the newcomer Thoreaux without a moment's hesitation. His right arm almost took Thoreaux's head off with one swing of the saber. Pro's second in command barely dodged the attack before letting off another pulse shot.

It went wide right, but then Caesar was back on his feet. His right leg was cut deeply, yet he thrust forward with Thoreaux at his side. Although gravely wounded, the man-beast wasn't stupid. He parried with his right arm, blocking Caesar's strike, at the same time taking massive steps toward the portal.

The cavern was vibrating, so the portal was ready to transport.

Thoreaux was letting his MechPulse fire shot after shot, and it was beginning to overheat. He'd have to switch to another weapon shortly, though Caesar wasn't sure there'd be time for that.

Prometheus still lay on the ground, not looking up, but Caesar could see that he was closer to the portal. It was pulling him.

Thoreaux was still backing the giant up. The man's right leg was now injured, having caught a pulse blast, but the MechPulse was done.

Thoreaux threw it to the ground, ripping a beam off his belt.

Caesar stopped going forward. His eyes remained on Prometheus. The Commonwealth had formed a ring around the portal and was slowly backing toward it. The man-beast now had protection. He'd fallen behind the ring, and Caesar could see him limping toward Prometheus.

He was going to take their leader through the portal.

Caesar understood he couldn't let it happen. Prometheus had to stay with them.

He rushed toward the Commonwealth line, both sabers alive in his hands. A Titan swung at him, but Caesar cut through his middle, the laser slicing metal and flesh alike.

Another tried for the gigante's head, but Caesar ducked, twirled, and thrust his saber in an uppercut. He caught the Titan just under the chin, the laser impaling his head. Caesar ripped it out without slowing, continuing toward his fallen leader.

The Titans that came at him couldn't handle the

gigante. He was too much for them, but he understood who he'd be facing again in a moment.

The man-beast had almost reached Prometheus. A Titan wearing a light-blue MechSuit was closing on him too. They were about five paces away.

Caesar couldn't see where anyone else was. The sounds of plasma and lasers and grunts and screams filled the air, whether Commonwealth or insurrection, he didn't know.

The man-beast grabbed Prometheus by his arm, lifting him and flipping him onto his shoulders. He still showed no sign of pain. His left arm and right leg hardly worked, yet the creature was carrying a man in a MechSuit as if it were nothing.

Time was up.

Caesar took two huge strides, launching himself into the air on the last one. He was aiming for the man-beast's back, hoping to break it. The light-blue Titan wasn't close enough to stop him, still being a meter or more away and retreating to the portal as well.

Just before Caesar hit the man-beast, he sidestepped as if he'd known the gigante was coming. Caesar hit the ground in a roll.

He tried to turn around, to gain purchase on the floor, but he couldn't stop the slide.

Caesar crossed the portal's plane and ceased existing on the planet Phoenix.

Thoreaux watched it all happen as a sick sense of doom spread through his mind.

It didn't matter how hard he fought, how many Commonwealth soldiers he brought down; he couldn't get to Prometheus.

He didn't have Caesar's strength or Pro's speed, and it was obvious that word had gone out for any Commonwealth soldiers to come to this portal if possible. They were flooding in, some not even attempting to fight Thoreaux's soldiers, simply rushing for the portal in a desperate bid to escape.

Prometheus' plan had worked. Thoreaux was getting reports from above, and the Commonwealth's armada was fleeing—what was left of it at least. They'd taken Phoenix, but now the Commonwealth was going to take Prometheus. Not on a dreadnought or some other Commonwealth-owned ship, but to a Commonwealth-owned *galaxy*.

Thoreaux's MechPulse lay on the ground. It had overheated, and he didn't have time to wait. Caesar had broken through the defensive line surrounding the portal, and Thoreaux was trying to cover his back, firing his beam at every Titan to come across his path.

It wasn't enough.

"Relm," he said into his comm. "Where are you?"

It took a moment, but Relm came back. "We just took the communication room. Where's Pro?"

Thoreaux's eyes widened, and he couldn't find any words to answer Relm.

"Thoreaux, you there?" Relm's voice was rising in panic.

Thoreaux said nothing. He raised his beam and fired over and over, trying to hit the mutant holding Prometheus. He was too far away.

Thoreaux ran forward, pulling a saber from his belt. He slit the first Titan he saw, but a mechanized elbow bashed him in the face, sending him sprawling across the floor. His vision blurred, but he managed to keep his eyes on Prometheus.

He watched as the mutant lifted his leader above his head and tossed him like a sack through the portal. The darkness reached up and snatched Thoreaux.

CHAPTER FOUR

The council, or what was left of it, met above the planet in the dreadnought Faitrin had commanded the battle from.

Thoreaux, Servia, Relm, Faitrin, and the AllMother.

Caesar, Prometheus, and Obs were gone. Thoreaux had replayed the holovid more than ten times, studying the disaster. The damned animal had been racing toward the Martian and was about to leap on the mutant's back when he threw Pro.

Obs had made a split-second decision, leaping with all his might at the portal. The two soul-bonded creatures crossed at the same moment. Wherever they were, they were together.

Aspen remained on Phoenix, helping organize the Terram's return to normality, or whatever semblance of it was possible.

Thoreaux wasn't concerned about the Terram at the moment, though. His thoughts were focused on Prometheus, and to a lesser extent, Caesar.

The right side of Thoreaux's face was bruised and

swollen. He couldn't see out of his right eye, but he hadn't been to the medbay yet. Faitrin had tried to convince him to take an hour to go get checked out, but he'd refused.

Two hours had passed since Prometheus, Obs, and Caesar had disappeared. The Commonwealth fleet had fled, and the ones who didn't get away fast enough were being hunted. Thoreaux had been told what happened when he fell unconscious: the Commonwealth soldiers had blitzed for the portal. Some of the insurrection's warriors had followed them through, but most had remained on Phoenix, unsure of what was on the other side and unwilling to find out.

Thoreaux was beyond angry at that, though he was keeping his rage inside for now. Their leader had gone through, so everyone should have followed.

He'd deal with that later.

"Jeeves, do we know where that portal leads?" he asked. The portals could be reprogrammed as needed, and the last portal that had been programmed for Phoenix had been destroyed when Pluto burned.

"No," the AI responded. "I'm still working with the Terram on it, but the destination was changed just before Prometheus crossed the portal's plane. This might be confusing, so let me break it down. The portal had three destinations. The first, the Commonwealth encrypted, so we can't know for certain, but we must assume it was Earth. The second destination lasted only three-point-two seconds, and there is zero data on where it was directed. The data isn't encrypted; it simply doesn't exist. The third destination flipped back to Commonwealth encryption."

"They're doing everything they can to keep us from

getting to him," Thoreaux whispered. The misdirects were just mind games. Thoreaux sat at a round table, and though he wanted to pace, the blood flow it caused in his head hurt entirely too much. He reached up with his left hand and gently rubbed the left side of his face. He stared at his feet as he spoke. "Servia, what are you thinking?"

The two of them had been one before Prometheus arrived. They'd been the AllMother's hands, doing her bidding without question. When Pro came, Servia's importance hadn't lessened, but Thoreaux's had grown. He had become the hands, and Servia had accepted it without a qualm.

Now, though, Thoreaux needed her.

She was quiet for a moment, sitting on the other side of the table. She was next to the AllMother. The older woman had not said anything since the group reconvened.

"Jeeves," Servia eventually asked, "what are the odds that Prometheus is dead?"

"Without his injury taken into account, I'd say very slim. Everything that is known about the Commonwealth and their current Imperial Ascendant leads me to believe he'll want a public execution. He'll risk a lot of lives to make that happen. I believe that wherever Prometheus is now, if he's not on Earth, he's heading there."

Servia looked at her fingers drumming on the table. Back and forth, starting at one pinkie, then traveling to the other before going back the way the wave had come. "Neptune. I think that's where we go. We program the portal, and we take our forces there."

Thoreaux had considered that. Neptune was the farthest planet from Earth, and it had a portal. He didn't know who ruled it, but they were Edge planets, which ruled themselves differently than the Sanctum planets. "What about our fleet?" he asked. "They can't get through the portal here."

Faitrin spoke then. "The gigantes can pilot the ships in the fifth dimension. Most of the ships can do long distances on autopilot, but for the parts where we need bodies, the gigantes can handle it. We send the fleet within the next day or so, and when we step through the portal, the ships will be waiting for us."

Thoreaux's eyebrows went up. That solved half his problems with going to Neptune. "Okay, so we go there. Then what?"

Servia, still drumming her fingers on the table, smiled. "We take it from whoever owns it." She looked up. "None of us are Prometheus, but if we're going to think like him, that's what he'd do because it's the last damned thing the Commonwealth would expect. They took our leader and one of our fiercest warriors. We should go into hiding, not take one of their planets."

Thoreaux leaned back in his chair and looked at the ceiling. "Jeeves, is that possible? Can you redirect the portal to get us to Neptune?"

"Yes, but we won't have much time," the AI answered. "The Commonwealth is constantly rerouting it, but if we move quickly, I should be able to hold the routing coordinates long enough."

Thoreaux didn't turn his head as he asked the next question. "AllMother, is Prometheus alive? Can you tell?"

It was the most important question he had asked. It was the only question that mattered. With the element of surprise, they might take Neptune. Thoreaux knew they would go no farther without Prometheus. If he was dead, so was this insurrection.

The AllMother's voice was firm. "He's alive, Thoreaux. Trust yourself, and keep trusting him. He's led us this far, and he delivered us the planet beneath us now. He's not done delivering us planets."

Thoreaux nodded. He didn't need to hear anything else. "Let's have one waiting for him when he gets back to us." He looked at Faitrin. "Get the fleet to Neptune." Turning to the rest, he said, "Prepare the troops. We're going through the portal."

CHAPTER FIVE

Ares was seated next to the robot he'd named Monk. Both were quiet. They'd just witnessed something they didn't understand or believe was possible.

The Commonwealth's fleet had been reduced by a third —blown up, burned out, and destroyed. What was left of them was fleeing through space. They were running away from the planet they'd captured. It was no longer theirs, which meant it was Alistair's.

The former Titan and the robot sat in something like a prison cell, waiting for the AllSeer to determine what was to be done with them both. According to Monk, the AllSeer had taken a break from his duties to watch the battle for Phoenix, allowing Monk to steal some time for the two of them.

"What's that mean?" Ares asked. "Did Alistair just win?"

Monk said nothing for a few moments, a rare silence since the robot always had a comeback ready. "It would appear," he eventually said, "that his insurrection won the planet."

Ares stared at the lifelike planet in front of him, flames covering the surface. "You think he might have died?"

"It's a possibility. Humans are awful judges of risk, and if I dare say so, you may be the most awful of all humans at it."

"Flattery will get you nowhere with me, Monk." Ares' eyes narrowed as he considered the likelihood of Alistair's death. He shook his head when he decided it wasn't possible. Too much had happened to bring him here with an algorithm inside his head. No, Alistair was alive.

The blue light on Monk's head was still shining. It was the only clue that a stealth shield was over this area, keeping prying eyes and ears from seeing or hearing what was happening.

Monk rolled to the center of the room, and when he touched the three-dimensional image of the planet, it disappeared. He turned to face Ares. "They'll be here shortly, the AllSeer's minions. Go ahead and stand up, put those clips back on you, and do your best to act as if nothing happened. I'll probably be led away shortly, but don't worry your pretty little head about it, Romulus."

Ares stood up and stretched his arms above his head, letting his muscles lengthen down to his toes. "What, me worry? That's not in my DNA, Monk. Just take care of yourself."

He slapped the clip on his legs and they froze. He lifted the clip for his wrists in Monk's direction. "Going to need your help here, pal."

The blue light atop Monk's head flashed red and the clip latched onto his wrists.

"See you in a bit, Romulus. Try your best not to get

killed during the intervening time. Despite you being you, you're now a valuable vessel, and I need to make sure you get where you're supposed to be going."

Veena had experienced something very different from Ares, or Monk for that matter. While Ares had been thrown in a brig of sorts, left to stand still because he was clipped, Veena was led to a private room.

The clips were removed, and while the door to her room closed, she opened it easily by simply commanding it.

Veena was a warrior, but she'd come from a powerful family, so she also knew the trappings of royalty. This room wasn't something the Imperial Ascendant would rest in back on Earth, but it wasn't far from it either.

She was naturally suspicious, given that Ares had been led off in clips, and she imagined that was where he remained. Veena couldn't do anything right now to get to her partner, but he was never far from her mind. While she had been afforded some luxuries, if she tried rushing into this bunker or whatever it was, all of them would be snatched away from her, which wouldn't enable her to help Ares or their mission.

She waited, knowing that sooner or later, someone would show up and tell some lie as to why she was being kept in these surroundings.

As Veena waited, her mind kept venturing to the AllSeer. For the first time since waking up on the machine world, she was focusing on something else other than her parents. Veena remembered when the Imperial Ascendant had brought her and Ares to that underground bunker. Back on Earth, before they'd been sent to find the Titan, before everything had gotten so fucked, she'd seen the other version of the creature who was now known as the AllSeer. She'd seen Alexander de Finita, first of his name. He'd been a remarkable specimen, perhaps the greatest physical version of man ever born or created, if that was how it had occurred.

The thing she'd seen when exiting the ship? Veena wanted to say there was some similarity between the two of them, but it was hard to do. The size, perhaps? Yes, both were large beyond nature, but the AllSeer dwarfed the man she'd seen back on Earth. His flesh had been covered with what looked like war armor, yet Veena didn't think that was it. The creature—and that was what she felt he was, not a man—had a machine-like quality. That war armor, that helmet, was doing more than protecting him from outside attack.

Veena thought it was holding him together.

She thought it might be part of him, something that couldn't be removed.

There were no clocks in the room, but Veena had a strong sense of standard time, and she knew it'd been around six hours when someone finally came.

The room had no panel to show her who was outside, and despite the thickness of the door, she heard someone approach.

It's not a person, Veena thought. *It's him. The AllSeer. The creature.*

The door opened, and he stood in front of her. He

seemed bigger now than he had before, as if he'd grown in the past few hours.

Veena scanned him, taking in every detail so she could replay it later.

What he wore did appear to be armor. Silver and black metal gauntlets adorned his hands and wrists. From there, the silver turned to green as the armor moved up his arms, though the black remained. The green was dark, and it flowed across his forearms and biceps in a way Veena didn't understand. Armor shouldn't work like that, at least not without decorative coverings over it, but that wasn't what she was looking at.

The rest of his body was similar, that green moving like a tide across his chest plate and legs. No skin was to be seen.

It was the helmet her eyes kept being drawn to.

The green waves looked like one of those Rorschach tests ancient psychologists used to use, making it hard to focus on the underlying black armor. It appeared to be form-fitting, like skin rather than plate armor, yet it would guard him against attacks.

He was twice her size, maybe more. Veena knew he could crush her with a slap. He could crush Ares with a slap, MechSuit or not.

She told herself this was a creature, not a man. If it had ever been a man, it was a long, long time ago.

"Where's Ares?" Veena asked.

"He's safe," the creature responded. He stepped farther into the room, and the door shut behind him. He walked over to the couch and placed his gauntlet-covered hand on the armrest. The metal clicked softly when his fingers touched the upholstery. "He'll continue to be safe until we reach Earth. After that, it will be his decision what happens." Slowly, gracefully even, the AllSeer sat on the couch. It sank under his weight, though he didn't seem to notice.

His eyes found Veena's. The irises were red like those of a mutant, the pupils as black as space, and the whites as pure as snow. Framed by dark armor, the look was unsettling.

"Veena de Ragnimus."

His voice was deeper than any she'd heard before, as if a beast that resided in his chest was doing the speaking for him.

"Do you believe in fate?" he asked.

Veena felt nothing but fear at that moment. She was staring at something beyond humanity, perhaps beyond even the gods. Had she not been in front of him, she wouldn't even have believed it possible. She didn't care if her voice betrayed her; there wasn't any way this creature would think she wasn't frightened. "I believe in honor."

The creature was silent for a long moment, then said, "It was fate that brought you to me. You and your companion, though for different reasons, I think. You can't imagine how long I've searched for you, how long I've waited for what's in your mind. You cannot possibly fathom it, but here you are."

His deep voice became soft, which Veena hadn't expected was possible.

"What do you want, Veena de Ragnimus? You went to the edge of the universe and conquered a planet that had kept me at bay for lifetimes. You left behind a world that was your home because of your honor. I'm not sure if anyone has asked you what you want, Veena?"

Staring at a mutant, the first to exist, Veena heard the question for the first time in her life. Truthfully? No. No one had ever asked her what she wanted. No one had cared, and outside of the few times she'd forced the question on herself, she'd been propelled by something or someone else.

Veena didn't know how it came over her.

Perhaps it was whatever the machines had done back on their planet. The continual thoughts of her parents, dead and gone, having left her alone for so much of her life. Maybe it was that she was on the outer stretches of the universe, her last partner wrenched away from her, or maybe she'd just had enough.

The tears came, and Veena saw her parents sitting on the couch in front of her. The mutant was gone, and through blurry eyes, she realized what she wanted. She didn't care who heard it. She didn't care how foolish she sounded.

"I want a family. I want a home."

CHAPTER SIX

Alistair opened his eyes to complete darkness.

He didn't move but lay as still as a predator stalking its next meal. He was on his back on something that felt hard. A table, perhaps.

His mind wasn't yet awake, so he understood little of where he was or how he'd gotten there. For an unknown reason, he knew he had to be careful of the left side of his body. It was damaged.

He did a quick mental scan of his body, checking it, and he felt no pain.

His brain warmed up, and memories slowly came back to him: The battle, Gracilis piercing his shoulder with the saber, The walk to the portal, and the fight with Caesar's group.

He'd passed out from pain, and that was the last thing his mind could tell him.

Now where am I? he wondered. If his shoulder wasn't painful, he was either on a lot of drugs or someone had patched him up.

Very carefully and slowly, he checked each of his limbs. Nothing stopped him from moving, so he hadn't been physically restrained.

Turning his head left and right, he tried to look around the room, but everything was black. Not a speck of light existed in this place. Human eyes were not built for this type of darkness.

Alistair figured he was being monitored, regardless of how black the room was, so he slowly moved his arms outward until his hands found the end of the table. He noted that his left arm had no limit in its range of motion, so clearly it wasn't just drugs in his system. Someone had fixed the injury.

Alistair turned, then sat up and swung his legs off the table. He used his hands to look for what held it up but found nothing, so it was floating. That meant wherever he was, they'd mastered the manipulation of gravity. They were minimally technologically efficient.

He stepped down from the table and found solid ground beneath him.

If they were monitoring him, there wasn't any reason to be quiet. They knew he was awake and up.

"My name is Alistair Kane. Show yourself. There's no need for this darkness."

A light flashed to his left. It was in the corner of the room and didn't illuminate much. It had a handle at the bottom and three concentric circles moving up the stick, each one smaller than the last, with the top being the smallest. The light shone gold, and he could see the hand holding it.

The person wore a robe, and as Alistair scanned the

holder, it was hard to tell much about them. The robe covered their entire body, including their head, and the light didn't illuminate beneath the cowl.

"We know your name," the stranger said.

"You're with the Commonwealth?" Alistair asked.

"We serve no man, only the gods."

That was the strangest thing Alistair had ever heard. It was so crazy, Alistair felt a chill roll down his back. People spoke of the gods, yes. They believed they existed, but humanity was no longer so arrogant as to think the creatures cared about the smallness of humans. No one prayed to the gods, and certainly, no one served them.

"Where am I?" he said, his voice colder than before.

"Earth would call this place WD-987," the shadowed figure answered, "but we need no name."

This was getting him nowhere, and the man clearly couldn't function logically.

"Okay," Alistair said, hating not being able to see. He sent his mind out, wanting to search the planet himself, but was blocked by the room. He slammed against all four walls and the ceiling with everything he had but felt no give.

"Your mental powers will only do what they're allowed, Alistair Kane. There is no need to try using them. The gods control this place, not humans."

Alistair crossed his arms, realizing he was wearing a cloak similar to the stranger's. "Look, you can keep playing this little game of half-answers and such, but I'm not sure why you're doing it. I'm not dead, which means you don't want to kill me. Are you just going to stand there and let me ask you questions?"

"We didn't come to get you, Kane. You were sent to us. There is no reason to kill you since we're all going to die very shortly. The gods have decided our time is finished, and it appears they've decided your time is over as well. You may die however you want, with dignity or acting as your kind does, but you are going to die." The stranger took a step closer. "I'm not playing games. I will answer any questions you ask, but I don't think you're going to like the answers. Let's not do these things here, though. Follow me, and we can find more suitable surroundings."

The stranger turned and began walking toward the far left. The light barely lit up a few feet around him, so Alistair couldn't see much of the room. That didn't matter, though. They were done here.

Alistair hustled forward, catching up with the small man. He was nearly the size of the Terram, which made Alistair wonder if they were underground. They walked through a doorway that Alistair had to duck under, which strengthened his suspicions.

If they could block his mind, he couldn't begin to know what their technological abilities were. Humans could block the mutants' mental abilities, but if the mind was strong enough, as the AllMother's had been, those blocks eventually failed.

The hall was as dark as the room had been. The only things illuminating Alistair's way were the three circles in front of him. Everything else was black.

Alistair went out of his body again in the hallway to see how far he could get. He went about a meter in front of him, then met the block. As he kept walking, following the stranger, the block remained in place at one meter around him. It didn't shrink or expand.

"You may continue to try, but you're going to find that I'm not lying," the stranger said from up ahead.

Alistair said nothing in response, just kept trying to expand his mind but got the same result. The stranger remained a constant two meters in front of him, never looking back, apparently having no fear of Alistair.

The walk wasn't far, but it was clear that this wasn't a home. It was either a building of some sort with short doorways, or they were in underground tunnels.

The stranger turned left and stepped through a doorway. Alistair stopped outside and peered in. He saw another room with no light, which was weird to say the least. The small lamp the stranger carried now sat on a table, just barely lighting the edges of it. It was circular and small, with enough room for four people.

The stranger was already in a chair, though Alistair couldn't see it.

He walked into the room and carefully made his way to the table, feeling with his hands for a second chair. He found one, sat, and stared at the shrouded man.

They weren't Commonwealth; Alistair believed that. He'd deal with the darkness in this place in a minute. There were more pressing matters. "You'll answer my questions, right?"

The stranger nodded.

"How did I get here?"

"You arrived through our portal."

"Was I injured?"

The stranger nodded again.

"Was I wearing armor?"

Nod.

That meant he'd gone directly from Phoenix to this place. There had likely been no other stops. "Was anyone with me?"

"You came alone."

He remembered what he'd done just before passing out. He'd pulled his Whip from Gracilis' belt and hooked it on his. "Was there a weapon on that armor?"

"Yes."

A primal urge to get his Whip back washed over Alistair. "Do you have it?"

"I do not, but if you mean to ask is it here, then yes, it is."

Alistair knew that if he lost his Whip, he would never get another. If it was gone, it was gone forever. It was here, though, on this planet, and that was enough for now.

Alistair sighed and leaned back in his chair. "How far are we from the Commonwealth's stronghold? Earth's Solar System?"

"I only know of the Commonwealth. I've heard of Earth, but to be honest, outside of learning their names, this is the first time I've thought about either."

That was nearly as strange a comment as what he'd said about the gods. Humans across the universe knew the Commonwealth, knew Earth. It was where humanity had sprung from, the species' homeworld. No matter how far from Earth one was, that still mattered.

This man was beyond strange, and Alistair imagined the rest of his little tribe was too. "Do your people have a name?"

He thought he saw a hint of a smile beneath the man's hood.

"People. That's a very odd word to use here. There have never been people here. You are the very first." The stranger reached up and slowly pulled his hood off his head.

Alistair, a man trained his entire life to not show his emotions because doing so could lead to his death, found he was unable to control his face. His eyes widened, his mouth dropped momentarily, and terror struck him. The only question that mattered came to his mind, then emerged from his mouth. "Are you engineered?"

The creature, because this was no man, shook his head.

The only other word that could describe something like this was one that humanity had long ago agreed wasn't real. Despite the innumerable stars and rocks that surrounded them, there had been no other life in the universe. No other species besides humans and the other lifeforms found on Earth.

Humanity was indeed alone in the universe, despite the improbability of that.

At least until now, because if this thing wasn't engineered, then it was an alien.

A chuckle came from the thing's odd mouth; it was obviously laughing at the look on Alistair's face. "What you see here isn't my true form. I'm not sure you could handle what I look like. This is the best I could do on short notice when one of you showed up here."

It was somewhat humanoid in appearance. Alistair saw two arms and two legs, though he couldn't see what lay beneath the robe. The head was round, or perhaps oval, and the skin completely smooth like a balloon slick with oil. The skin was the whitest Alistair had ever encountered, the whitest *thing* he'd ever seen. It was as if sunlight had never touched it.

There were no ears, just holes in the side of its head, and the mouth was much too small for his head, as if perhaps there'd been a mistake made in the womb.

The eyes were by far the strangest. No eyebrows, no eyelashes. No *eyes*. Just empty holes. If you took the eyes out of the picture, it looked like someone who only vaguely knew what a human looked like had hastily tried to put one together.

Given the eyes in the picture, it was horrifying.

"If you just changed into this form, why don't you put some eyes in your head?" Alistair asked, unnerved.

"None of our kind has sight, Kane. We cannot see. The eyes were too foreign for me to think about or create in the short time I had. More, I didn't care. Death is near. Our time is nearly up."

The questions in Alistair's mind were increasing to the point of being endless. "Why can't you see in your original form? How do you operate without sight? Why do you keep saying we're going to die?"

The creature didn't blink. There were just dark holes on a milk-white face. He did smile with his small mouth, though. To Alistair, it looked like a smile you'd give a young child after they'd asked something cute but dumb. "Two of your questions have one answer. We are dying because our star is nearly a supernova, but it will fail and turn into a black hole. We have not seen light for many generations, but the gods are good. We can operate, as you call it, because of our mental capabilities. Given your nature, I believe you can understand that."

The questions about this creature left Alistair's mind. Luna, Thoreaux, Servia, Caesar, and the rest replaced this alien. "How long before it turns into a black hole?"

"Who can say? It's not important. What you mean to ask, Kane, is how long do we have before we die, correct?"

Alistair nodded. His fear was gone. Prometheus was knocking, wanting out, though Alistair understood this wasn't the time nor the place. He nodded at the creature.

"On your time scale, we have about two weeks before life can no longer be sustained. We've continually increased our defenses against the star, but they can no longer hold. They're failing us, and you'll understand that as you walk our home."

Alistair wanted to stand, but he knew he couldn't find his way around this place. "I'm good with walking your grounds. Where's the portal? If you have one, you must know how to send me somewhere else. It's time for me to go."

"You're not leaving. The gods brought you to us, and that means your fate is to be the same as our own. That was what they willed, so that's what will happen. Acceptance is what your species lacks. Your refusal to accept what happens to you causes all your suffering. The gods even sent you a messenger who said those exact words long ago. Multiple messengers. However, your kind continues to refuse. Alistair Kane, you have two weeks left to live. Use them wisely. Use them to accept that fact, and your time here will be easier."

CHAPTER SEVEN

Hector and his grandfather Caius stood before the Imperial Ascendant. It was Hector's first time entering the throne room, though he knew Caius had been there before.

Hector had nearly refused medical attention, wanting the broken bones and scarred flesh he'd received to be a reminder for future battles. His grandfather had very patiently explained why that couldn't be. His perfection would lead men better than his scars, and if he needed a reminder of his loss in battle, he only need ask where Alistair Kane was.

The two de Gracilises had already done the appropriate kneeling and One-People-One-Purpose formalities. Hector's face looked as it had before he'd left Earth. He'd fought Prometheus and somehow lost. Even when he thought he'd lost the battle but won the war, the man had proved to be invincible.

That was why they were in front of Alexander de Finita. He'd given Hector three days to heal, and for most men, that would have taken a month. Hector wasn't most men, though, and when the Ascendant called, he answered.

He wanted to know what had happened.

He wanted to know how they'd lost, though he had every report on the matter.

De Finita wanted to hear it from Hector's mouth, and because he knew the unspoken game the two were playing, he wanted Caius there as well.

The Ascendant appeared calm, sitting in a chair that was two meters above the Martians. He looked as if two bugs had just crawled into this room. They were beneath him, but he wasn't a cruel man, so he would watch as they crawled about in the dirt.

"Gentle sirs, I think it's time to stop the charade," he said from his perch. "Especially after what happened on Phoenix. There is a mutant before me, one made by his grandfather. I am not sure how he managed to keep the red out of your eyes, but you are a mutant all the same. Does anyone here dare deny that to the Imperial Ascendant?"

Hector didn't look away, not for a second, nor would he lie to this man about anything. It wasn't out of loyalty to the Commonwealth or the Ascendancy, but his honor. He'd already lied to this man when his honor called for it, thus the sham marriage he'd been forced into. Hector would die before losing his honor.

Hector had never denied what he was, not even to himself. From a young age, his father and grandfather had explained the reasons for his modifications, and Hector hadn't thought badly of the procedure or those who gave it to him.

He'd become greater than every other man born, and in

his mind, the only reason mutants were banned was because the weak feared them.

Neither Hector nor Caius said anything. Silence filled the room.

"Good." His eyes fell on Caius. "We'll discuss certain things regarding that little revelation in the future, but for now, I want to know how the greatest mutant I've ever seen backed by the force of the strongest government ever to be created controlled a planet that had a wall of fire as its atmosphere lost to a group of rebels formed within a few months?"

Hector hadn't been allowed much time with his grand-father. A stealth machine was useless since the Ascendant had kept someone next to each of them nearly every moment of the day, and especially when the two were together. He didn't know how his grandfather wanted him to respond, nor could Caius respond for him.

Hector wouldn't lie. "We underestimated our opponent in every way. We thought our fleet would defeat his. We thought our control of the planet would keep him from gaining control. We thought our warriors better than his. In every way, we underestimated him, and if I can speak freely, my Liege, we overestimated ourselves. I include myself in this."

The Ascendant showed no emotion, but his question had told Hector what he wanted. It was a simple question but profound. He wanted Hector and Caius to understand their weaknesses.

"Tell me, how did you underestimate him?"

Hector had thought of nothing else since he'd stepped through the portal, thinking he would see the unconscious

Kane lying in front of him. He'd seen nothing but the Ascendant and his guard.

"I allowed no assistance, thinking I could best him alone. I'm faster and stronger than him, but the first thing I underestimated was his skill, my Liege. Despite my speed and strength, it felt like he knew what I was going to do before I did it. I've never seen anyone fight like him, and until three days ago, I honestly didn't think that much skill could be attained."

The Ascendant raised an eyebrow, his first movement. "Is that all?"

Hector shook his head. "Speaking only of myself and not the failures of the overall strategy, I didn't think the man had the heart he did. I didn't think he had the sheer determination. Again, being honest with you, my Liege, the only man I know with a stronger resolve than my own is my grandfather, and I don't consider mine much less than his. I think Alistair Kane's may be greater than both of ours, and I didn't account for it."

For the first time since they'd entered the room, Alexander looked genuinely curious. The rest of this had been for show, to rub their noses in the shit they'd created. Alexander only allowed a bit of what he was thinking to appear on his face; the man was the Ascendant, after all. Yet, it was enough for Hector to see it. He wanted to hear more about the last part.

"Expand on that if you will," Alexander said. "What do you mean by his determination?"

Through his operation and healing time, the warrior had done no reading. He'd not spoken to anyone, not even his sham wife. He'd thought only about his failure, and he'd done it clinically. He understood that no good would come from self-flagellation. It would not help him win the next time he saw Kane. He dissected everything his eyes had seen, his mind remembering the majority of it. In his head, he kept replaying Kane's actions, movements, and even body language. He studied him, trying to come to know him in a way he'd ignored last time.

"I've killed many people, my Liege. Men and women, anyone who came against me. I've seen people of all ages die from every imaginable kind of wound. Normally, when that wound comes, the one that's going to end their life, they give up. I've seen it with animals too. The fight in them dissipates because they know it's over." The memory started replaying inside his head. He'd been on the ground. Kane had rushed forward, then leaped to come down on top of Hector. The Martian was too quick, pushing the Whip away, then driving his weapon through the former Titan. "I gave him a wound that should have killed him. I cut through him. I was not a hand's width from his heart. At that point, most men would have rolled over and died, or tried to run even though a laser had been shoved through their body. Kane didn't do either of those. He bashed me in the head with his helmet until I was unconscious. In my experience, there aren't men born like him. Not in the Commonwealth, and most likely not outside of it either."

The Ascendant was quiet for a little over a minute, his eyes never breaking from Hector's. "It sounds like you at least respect him and perhaps fear him, de Gracilis? Which of those is it?"

Hector didn't need a moment to consider this question.

"I've never met a man worthy of killing. He's the first. I respect him, and I won't underestimate him again. I'm unsure if I'm capable of feeling fear. It's not something I'm acquainted with."

"Perhaps you *are* incapable of it," the Ascendant responded, "or you will be soon. I've one more question for you. From everything I've seen and read, Kane was using his mental powers to destroy our fleet. While he was fighting you, he was also controlling the planet's air defense system. Were you aware of that?"

Hector nodded.

"Some might say that he fought you with one arm tied behind his back and still won. Truthfully, he didn't kill you because the Titan at your side kept him from doing so. Let's say that the next time you encounter him, he doesn't have an armada to kill and can use all of his powers against you? Do you think you can win?"

Hector had considered the question honestly. Physically, he was superior to Kane, but the mental abilities the man possessed were far beyond anything Hector had ever encountered. Still, it wasn't a hard answer for the Martian.

"My Liege, I didn't mention his mental powers in my report because I know the man now. I won't underestimate him again, and the next time he sees me, it will be the last time he sees anyone."

"Well, let's hope so," Alexander said, "because I don't think your dear old grandfather here is going to be able to whip up any more mutants like you by the time Kane is on our doorstep."

The Ascendant stood, descended from his chair, and strode between the two of them. Hector and Caius moved out of the way. The Ascendant kept moving forward, and when his back was to them, Hector caught his grandfather's eye. The man gave the slightest nod, but Hector understood. Caius approved of how he'd handled the situation.

"While I'm sure you're going to miss your wife, Hector," Alexander called from a few meters in front of them, swiftly moving across the throne room, "I'm afraid you won't be able to stay with her. We still aren't sure where Kane went when he passed through the portal, though our engineers did a fantastic job of allowing us to control it off-world. We're looking for Kane, and eventually, we'll find out where he went, but for now, we need to focus on the immediate threat."

He stopped at the wall. Hector and Caius stood just behind and on either side of him. The Praetorians lined the walls, none glancing at the three men but continuing to stare forward as they had the entire time.

The Ascendant touched a small button to the left, and a large screen lifted from the floor beneath him. It floated at the Ascendant's eye level, though Hector had to look down to see it.

"Kane's army is heading to our Solar System. We're almost sure Kane isn't with them, which means they don't know where he is either, yet they've decided to continue the insurrection."

His hand darted over the screen, and a trail of ships outlined in neon green appeared on it. "That's his fleet, the entirety of it. They're moving in the fifth dimension, so no humans are aboard, but his mercenary army controls it. We can't keep up with them, but we imagine they're a few days out at this point since the gigantes can fly in the fifth dimension with no problem." He touched the screen once more and the planet Phoenix appeared, though at a fair distance. "We have one scout ship still watching the planet. We saw them unload anyone not a gigante onto the planet, so right now, they're waiting for the fleet to arrive. We still control the portal."

With an angry look, the Ascendant shook his head.

"They tell me the Subversives can regain control of it, at least for a time. The best intelligence we have says they're heading for Neptune, which is a smart move. The planet is the farthest from Earth, and those out there have less allegiance to the Commonwealth than those closer in. After your loss on Phoenix, our fleet has had enough time to get back, obviously, as well as those who managed to escape through the portal. Right now, Neptune is preparing their defenses. The option of destroying the portal has been mentioned, but I'm not going to do that."

He turned so he was facing the Martians.

"I'm not going to hide from these Subversives, good sirs. The Commonwealth has stood for a thousand years, and we've never hidden from anything. The Commonwealth allowed men to travel the stars. The portals they're using came from us, from our ingenuity, from my ancestors, so we will let them come through the portal, then we will cut them down." His eyes found Hector's. "You're going to be on the front line, Hector de Gracilis. If it's glory you look for, then I'll give you another chance because it's clear you didn't get it at Phoenix."

Hector understood what that meant. The frontal assault at the portal would be a bloodbath, a massacre. The birds would eat for days from that one battle. The dead would be uncountable, and the Imperial Ascendant meant for Hector to be among them.

"When do I leave?" he asked.

"The ship has been ready for an hour. They're waiting for you."

"Is Aletheia accompanying me?"

Alexander nodded. "Of course. If Kane shows up, I want to make sure someone is there to save you."

Alexander wondered what the old man, Caius, was thinking. His greatest chance of overthrowing the Ascendancy and assuming it for himself had just lost a battle to an inferior warrior. Even Hector had mentioned the two weren't equally matched. Did Caius still think he could do it, or was he doubting his plan now?

Either way, Alexander was no longer worried about him.

His main concern was what had happened to Kane. It made no sense, and as he headed to the Fathers, he hoped they'd found an answer.

The battle at Phoenix had been a disappointment and a large one. It seemed that whatever Alexander did, Kane had a countermove, and truthfully, Hector's evaluation of the battle had been accurate. They continued to underestimate the man, and Alexander couldn't deny that he'd done it from the beginning. He just hadn't been able to fathom that such a person could exist, but as Hector said, he did.

Alexander was done underestimating him.

He rose above the throne room to where his ancestors awaited him.

Alexander bowed. "One People. One Purpose." He straightened when he was done and placed his hands behind his back.

The orb's light contracted to a tiny point. All the voices spoke as one, but this time, they weren't scornful of Alexander. "We can't find him."

It was a simple answer that showed the Fathers' frustration.

"What does it mean? Did someone else gain control of the portal for a few moments just when Kane was tossed through?"

"There are possibilities here we can't account for. The traces left by the change in portal direction aren't anything we've seen before. It wasn't human."

Alexander raised one eyebrow. "There's some other force in play here. The question is, is it on our side or his?"

"To assume it's on our side would be a grave error if we're wrong," the orb answered. "It's against us. Kane lives, and we don't know where he is."

"Do you know the likelihood of him being on Neptune when the force arrives?" Alexander asked.

"It's impossible to say without knowing where he is now. The best thing we can hope to do is destroy his forces on Neptune. If he returns after that, it won't matter."

Alexander was quiet for a few moments and looked at his feet. "Fathers, in the beginning, you were right. I thought this would be a simple exercise even when you told me it wouldn't. I was arrogant and thought one man couldn't stand against us. I see it now, and I apologize to you all. I won't make those mistakes again. If this man beats us, if he brings down the Commonwealth, it won't be because I underestimated him." He looked up. "I'm going to assume he'll be on Neptune and that he's going to show up when most needed. I'm going to assume he will be healthy and ready to kill. If we make those assumptions, what are the odds that he wins?"

The orb said nothing as it digested what Alexander had given it.

"Fifty percent."

"If he conquers Neptune, what happens to our odds on the next planet?"

"Fifty-two and a half percent chance he wins there. After that, his odds begin to drop because his forces will be depleted with each planet he conquers."

Alexander shook his head. "That would be an underestimation of his ability. What if he rallies people to his banner and they forsake ours? Then his forces will grow with each victory. It's possible his odds could increase."

"With those variables, his odds increase drastically," the orb responded. "What is going on with the plans of ensuring our survival, regardless of what happens?"

"They're continuing apace. I'll have an update for you in the next few days. I'm not worried about that point."

The orb chuckled. "Underestimation again, Alexander, but this time it's not for Kane. Whatever is at work here, whatever transferred that Titan to a place we can't see, it could very well be a force that wants to stop our future survival. It may want to destroy the AI apparatus that allows us to exist. Do not think it isn't possible, or you might doom your ancestors and everything we've built."

Alexander's eyes narrowed. He hadn't considered that possibility. "The AllSeer wouldn't want that to happen. He looks at this place as his birthright, himself as the natural successor."

"We're not talking about the AllSeer, Alexander. He's in our calculations, and we will talk about him momentarily. Whatever took Kane wasn't the AllSeer. We would have seen his traces in the data. It's something else, and perhaps it *doesn't* want our continued existence. That was the whole purpose of this plan—that no matter what happens, we can't be killed off as an entity. Maybe something wants that to happen."

Alexander didn't know what to say. It went back to the damned algorithm, but they knew nothing about it. Yet, the Fathers continued to worry about something that seemed so remote as to be impossible.

None of this has seemed possible, Alexander thought. *Here you are, sending troops to Neptune to fight off a rebellion that spans galaxies. Maybe they're right.*

"We'll continue our efforts," he said. "Now, what of the AllSeer?"

"He's coming too," the orb answered.

Alexander scoffed. "Here? To Earth?"

"Yes. We are one hundred percent certain about that. While his home planet is out of our reach, we know his psyche as well as we know any de Finita's. There is no way the AllMother and her rebellion will return to Earth, and he is coming."

"Right now, we're massing our forces on Neptune, not here. Earth is the most vulnerable it's been in one thousand years," Alexander said. "If he comes now, he takes Earth."

Softly, the orb spoke. "Calm down. If we thought that would happen, we would have dealt with this much earlier. The AllSeer, in all probability, is insane. He is obsessed with the AllMother. His insanity tells him he must reunite with her before he can take back his birthright. He won't attack Earth before he has her."

Alexander looked at the ceiling as he thought about that. "The old woman won't stay on Phoenix. There she'd be exposed to the AllSeer. She'll be on Neptune, and the AllSeer will show up next." He looked at the orb. "Capturing her is key to getting the AllSeer where we want him. I'll make sure that happens."

"That's exactly right, Alexander. If we control the woman, we control her brother."

CHAPTER EIGHT

When Veena had finished crying and the mutant left, she could hardly believe what she'd done and said.

She'd opened up to that thing in a way she'd never opened up to anyone else. Not to anyone in the academy, not to her underlings in the Commonwealth, not even to Ares.

Veena didn't understand it, yet once she let that emotion out into the world, she couldn't deny the truth of it.

That mutant had asked her what she wanted, and she hadn't lied. She wanted a home. She wanted a family. She wanted not to be alone any longer. The wars, the glory, the conquest—none of that mattered to her any longer, if it ever really had. She realized now that those things had only been substitutes for her parents.

They'd filled a hole she couldn't admit existed.

Two days had passed since she'd last seen the mutant or anyone else. The door to her quarters opened when she wanted it to, and it appeared that she was free to go wherever she wanted, though she never left.

Food, drink, even laundry had been delivered to her. Veena felt more like a guest than a prisoner, and she didn't like that.

Where was Ares? What had happened to him?

She was struggling mightily with going to look for him. She knew he already would have left this room to find her, but he was brash where she was calculating. If Veena left, the mutant and all his minions would know. They'd see her every move; she wouldn't get to Ares unless they wanted her to, and then what?

There was no answer or nothing good at least.

She waited in her room for two days, wondering what came next.

Midway through the second day, the mutant arrived again.

He entered her room, looking just as large as she remembered. She knew what they called him: the AllSeer. She had been on her bed when she saw him outside the door, and she jumped to her feet as she would if he'd been a superior officer in the Commonwealth. It wasn't that she thought of him as a superior, but she didn't want him to see her lying in bed.

He stepped through the door, wearing the same armor as before. Veena felt small next to this massive animal. She imagined the first humans to see dinosaur skeletons had felt similar.

"Where's Ares?" she asked without hesitation. She didn't know what her voice sounded like to the animal, but there wasn't anything she could do about the fear he inspired. She wanted to know where her friend was.

"He's alive. He hasn't been harmed," the AllSeer said.

"That wasn't what I asked. Where is he?"

"He's aboard the ships. That's why I'm here. It's time for us to leave this planet. You'll be coming as well, and I'd like to spend more time with you on our journey."

Veena's brow furrowed. "Where are we going?"

"Do you know why people lie, Veena?" the mutant asked, but he didn't wait for an answer. "They lie because they're scared. That's it. There's no other reason for it. I am one of the few people ever to exist who doesn't know fear. I've never known it, not even before my father's mutation of me. Now? After all these years, I can hardly understand what it is. I say that because I want you to know I'll never lie to you."

Veena did her best to show no emotion, though internally she scoffed at the notion. Yet as she thought about it, there was logic in it. He didn't fear her. Why would he?

"We are going to get my sister, then from there, we're going to Earth. You know my story, I presume?"

Veena nodded.

"I'm curious," the mutant said. "What are the stories about me on Earth?"

Veena was quiet for a moment, remembering the things she'd heard but that no one spoke of. At least, they weren't supposed to, but she'd heard them, hadn't she? "You're a rumor, and so is your sister. No one knows what happened to the two of you, but the official line is you're dead. When we were sent to find Alistair Kane, the Ascendant—"

The AllSeer interrupted her. "His name is Alexander, right?"

"Yes, he's the second of his name. It's known that you were the first."

The AllSeer nodded. "My apologies for interrupting. Please, continue."

"We were being sent after Kane, and the Ascendant took us to this room I didn't know existed. Did he show us the original you or the cloned you? I don't know which. The body in the vat was still alive, both of them. That's when he told us the truth, that you existed and the official line was a lie. You two were the first mutants. On Earth, your name is only whispered, as is your sister's."

The AllSeer still stood just inside the door, not venturing closer. "You and I are more alike than you can imagine, Veena. My family abandoned me. My father used me to see what he could accomplish. I was just a boy then, seventeen years old. What could I know about life or the future? At seventeen, you're going to live forever. When my father discovered that what he created wasn't what he wanted, he didn't try to fix it; he simply discarded us. My name cannot be spoken, and neither can my sister's, though I was the rightful heir to the throne. The current lineage is a bastardization of what was meant to happen. My sister fled, as did I, and I've been alone ever since. No family. No home. Not until I built this, but if you had left your room, you'd see that this could never be a human's home."

He looked at the floor and shook his head sadly.

"My home is Earth, and I'm going back to it. You and the one you call Ares are coming with me."

He looked up again. "Do you know why I'm bringing you? Do you understand what happened on the machine world?"

The fear had left Veena. She hadn't realized when it happened, but it had. The mutant had somehow disarmed her by talking about his life. When she spoke, it wasn't like speaking to a monster, but a human. "They put the algorithm in my head. You want it. Where did the machine world come from? How was it even there?"

The AllSeer shrugged, his massive shoulders moving like boulders around his neck. "I have theories, but I don't know if they're correct. There's no one to bounce my ideas off, no one to speak to. All the decisions I make are mine alone. Perhaps the gods put it there, both the rock and the machines."

Veena rejected the idea. "If the gods exist, they don't care about us. They care about us as much as they care about the insects that walk on your planet."

A smirk appeared on the black-armored face in front of her. "You didn't create those insects. If the gods created us, certainly they must care. If they didn't create us, then how did those machines get out there? More, why did they protect the algorithm for so many years but have finally put it in your mind, yours and your friend's?"

Veena didn't have an answer, and though she'd asked the question, she didn't care about philosophizing more. The mutant didn't know, and neither did she, so there wasn't any point in going on about it. "What do you want with the algorithm?"

"It's owed to me. The algorithm and the AI it created."

The AllSeer cocked his head to the left. "Do those on Earth know about the Fathers?"

With a raised eyebrow, Veena shook her head. "The rumor is that there was some sort of powerful AI, and someone stole the algorithm that created it. We went searching for the algorithm because we had no other choice. We were dead-broke and being hunted. The algorithm could buy us freedom, or that's what we thought."

Why am I telling him all this? Veena wondered. She was still disarmed, and this mutant was willing to give her information. Rather than clamming up, Veena was reciprocating. She didn't understand it but was doing it anyway.

"The Fathers are my progenitors going down the line, with each Ascendant being loaded into the artificial intelligence you speak of. Besides my father, who is still alive inside that AI, I am their ancestor." He paused and nodded at Veena. "With what's in your head, I can ensure the artificial intelligence survives forever or destroy it and restart it. What happens depends on what the Fathers want to do and whether they support my rise to the throne that is rightfully mine. If they don't, then we restart. We do it again, only better this time."

"I'm assuming I have no choice in any of this?" Veena asked. "This nice room, the door that is never locked, the food. None of it extends to me having a choice about what I want to do, right?"

"Only in this one area. The machines gave you the algorithm, and once I have my sister, I will need it. Other than that choice, the rest are yours. Where you want to go. What you want to do. You'll have access to the ship the same as any Myrmidon."

"I want to see Ares," Veena demanded.

"You will in time," he responded softly. "Right now, though, we need to get you moved to my ship and prepared for travel. I won't be with you all the time, but I'd like to see you once a day or so, Veena. The time of my rising is nearly here, and I think you have a place in it, an important place."

He was silent for a moment.

"Someone will be here to get you momentarily. I appreciate your cooperation in these matters. These are exciting times, which have been building for a thousand years. I'm glad you're here to witness it."

The AllSeer left the room quickly. Despite his monstrous size and demonic mien, Veena felt that for a few seconds, he'd been vulnerable. She didn't see how that was possible. There wasn't anything to be vulnerable about in that mutant, but it'd been there. He hadn't been lying when he'd told her he was glad she was here.

What are you? Veena wondered. *Are you mankind's savior or our doom? Are you insane or do you simply want what is rightfully yours?*

Ares and Monk had been transferred to the AllSeer's dreadnought hours previously. The clip on Ares' ankles had been removed, while the ones on his wrists had been dialed down. He could move. He could feed himself. He could talk.

Monk had been with him at times over the past few

days, and other times, Myrmidons came for him and took him away.

Now the two were in one of the dreadnought's brigs. The Myrmidon who'd brought them had removed Ares' wrist clip, which likely meant they were going to be traveling in this ship for a long while. The brig, as well as everything else Ares had seen during his time with the AllSeer's group of psychopaths, was very different than what he'd seen before.

It appeared to be endless.

Ares didn't know how that was possible, but that was the only way he could describe it. He wasn't locked into a cell as he'd been when Alistair had captured him. He could roam freely in the brig. There were doors, chairs, tables, beds, and room after room. Ares found himself walking through what seemed to be a ship unto itself.

Monk was brought in about an hour later. He was silent as the Myrmidon stepped out of the brig, though Ares didn't understand how that was possible because *he* sure as Hades couldn't do it.

"This thing is endless," he told Monk as he stared after the Myrmidon. The door quickly shut, locking him in. He didn't look at Monk but kept staring at where the Myrmidon had exited.

He stepped toward the door. It opened automatically, but the scene beyond it was different. He was in another room like the one he currently stood in. A bed, a table, a chair. No warship. "I don't know how they do it, but it's endless."

Monk rolled into the new room and looked it over. It

appeared to be metal, but there was a sponginess to the ship that said the material was something different.

"It's not endless," Monk said as his treads rolled around to face Ares. "It's simply a moving brig. It's probably only three rooms right now, though they could make it larger. The rooms just reorganize themselves at a pace faster than you can move or even see. The AllSeer likes his tricks, and this is one of them. A person spends enough time in here without seeing anyone else, they could lose their mind."

Ares stepped into the new room. The door closed behind him immediately. "He wants me insane before this is over?"

Monk nodded and sounded more cavalier than Ares liked when he said, "Probably. You have no use for him outside of that single thing in your mind. If you're insane, you'll be much easier to manage when we get to Earth."

Ares sighed, walked over to the bed, and sat on it. It also had the spongy feel of the floor, which he didn't like one bit. Sleeping on this thing wouldn't be pleasant. "What have they been doing with you?"

"They're trying to crack my core code." Monk rolled over to the table and brushed his hands across it. "We could play cards here to pass the time."

"You have cards?"

The front part of Monk's face lit up, and a holodeck of cards flashed to the middle of the table.

"Ha. You'll know all the cards. You'll cheat."

The cards disappeared, and Monk turned. "I wouldn't cheat to beat you. I wouldn't need to. I can keep us entertained, though. On the world where you found me, there was a lot of downtime. We found ways to keep ourselves busy."

"Back to my original question. Why aren't they still trying to crack your core code? Why do they let you come back here?"

"They're having trouble, mainly that cracking my core code will create a thermonuclear blast that would be like a supernova. There's no way to protect against it, and they can't find a way around it. The Myrmidon scientists get tired, so they send me back while they rest and argue amongst themselves. I don't know."

"Have they thought of torturing you?" Ares asked with a smile. "I'd enjoy that, I think."

"I'm sure you would, cretin, but it's hard to torture a being who doesn't sense pain. The main problem is that the AllSeer, for all his power and tricks, is still human. Whatever I am, I'm not that, so he can't figure me out."

The smile dropped from Ares' face. "Will he be able to?"

"If he had enough time, I'm sure he could, but my hope is that time is on my side. There isn't a lot I can do about it." The droid let out a long, loud mechanical sigh. "I wish the AllSeer's sexual preferences were different. I don't think Veena would ask as many questions."

Ares ignored the barb. "Have you seen her? Do you have any idea what's going on with her?"

"She's safe, Ares. She'll be safe until we get to Earth. Remember that. Neither of you can be hurt while he needs that algorithm."

"Only driven insane, right?"

Monk backed up so he was against the wall and staring straight forward. "This is going to be a long trip. Try not to be so obtuse. Plus, there are things I need to talk to you about that I haven't shared previously, so kindly shut up and listen."

The blue light on the top of his head flashed on, signaling they were under stealth protection.

"This ship isn't a ship. It's an organism, but it listens differently than the usual security apparatuses. I can block it for a time, but not forever, so don't ask too many questions." Monk turned his head to meet Ares' gaze. "Got it?"

Ares nodded.

Monk was quiet for a moment, which was odd for the machine. He never needed to gather his thoughts, yet he appeared to be doing so now.

"I didn't show you everything I saw on Phoenix because I couldn't risk you breaking down if your former leader died. It's possible that he will, and even if that happens, we must go on. Your purpose is different from his, and though they complement each other, we will go on no matter what. I kept a lot of what happened to myself." He paused to give Ares a moment to ask a question.

Ares didn't. Monk was probably right. Alistair's death, even now, would do more than shake Ares.

"Your silence is my favorite sound in the universe," Monk said. "I'm going to tell you what happened because we're going forward. I realize lies won't serve us well. Kane fought well against a vicious opponent. In some ways, he won the battle, and he certainly created the opportunity his insurrection grabbed to win the planet. Yet, in the end, his enemy got the better of him for reasons we don't have time to go into. I had a choice to make since the Commonwealth was taking him back to the Solar System, most likely to Earth. Once there, Kane's capabilities wouldn't matter. He'd never escape. The insurrection would end, and we'd have to go forward on our own. Trust me when I say this: the end of the insurrection would make our purpose *much* harder."

Monk sighed again, and this time it sounded human. It sounded as if he were unsure of himself? Maybe. Ares didn't know if the machine was programmed to produce shows of emotion, or if he did it to help humans relate to him. Ares kept his mouth shut about those questions. There'd be plenty of time for them later.

"My technical abilities surpass anything humans understand. You are a thousand years behind what I'm capable of doing. I had a choice to make: I could let Kane go to Earth, or I could reroute the portal to a place humans aren't aware of. I rerouted it for mere seconds, just enough time for Kane to escape the Commonwealth."

He slowly turned his head and looked at Ares.

"I might have made a mistake, or at least, I might not have saved him."

The damned machine paused. After long seconds, Ares asked, "Are you waiting for me to ask what in the fuck you did, or are you planning on telling me?"

"For the first time, you insufferable human, I might have made a mistake. I'm older than you can imagine, and I've never made a mistake before. I realize you can't fathom that since most of your existence consists of bumbling through horrible decision after horrible decision, but for a being like me, it's a lot to handle."

He looked at the floor.

"The place I sent him to is also an ancient civilization,

which was necessary to keep the Commonwealth away from him. Humanity doesn't know about it. A human would consider them to be of alien origin, yet they had the portal tech needed to move Kane. There wasn't any way the Commonwealth could get to him, and given what I know about the man, I thought he might be resourceful enough to return to his insurrection. I can hack the AllSeer's systems from time to time when they aren't operating on me or when they think I'm partially deactivated and leave me alone. I was briefly able to bridge to the civilization and download as much as I could."

He paused once again, something Ares hated.

"What I found out is less than perfect. The civilization I sent Kane to is facing an extinction-level event, and it seems that despite their technological advancement, they're okay with it. I don't understand. The species and their culture are mysteries to me too. Their tech is better than mine, and they detected me almost immediately. It was simple for them to thrust me out, then block me. There's no way back into their systems, at least not for me. However, what I was able to see showed that they are at peace with extinction and Kane is facing the same thing. They won't let him use their portal to leave. He will die with them."

Ares stood up, unable to help himself. "Alistair's going to die no matter what? How long does he have?"

"I didn't have time to figure that out," Monk said without looking up, "but there's more, so don't dirty your pants yet. The AllSeer sent some sort of *creatures* after Kane months ago. They're capable of fifth dimension travel and can apparently track Kane regardless of the distance.

At fifth-dimensional speeds, they'll reach the alien planet soon. If the extinction-level event doesn't kill him, they probably will. I can track them sometimes, using hacks on the AllSeer, which will give us insight into what's happening."

Ares closed his eyes, gritting his teeth. It was enough to know Alistair was going to die, but there'd been hope while he thought the man was alive. There'd been hope thinking that perhaps fate was involved here because he and Kane were heading to the same place. Both had the same goal: destroying the Commonwealth. If Alistair was gone? He didn't open his eyes as he asked, "What's that do to us, Monk? If Alistair isn't with his rebellion, what happens to it?"

"Without Kane, the insurrection is doomed. I don't know what they're planning right now, but it doesn't matter. They will lose. The AllSeer will get hold of the AllMother unless she's killed beforehand. If that happens, everything falls on you and me since I'm not so sure Veena is going to free herself from her parents' mental bonds." The machine shook his head slowly. "You're no Alistair Kane, and even he needed an army to push back the Commonwealth. I'm not sure what happens, only that the odds are greatly diminished."

Ares moved over to the wall on his left, put his forearm on it, and leaned his head against his arm. It wasn't his death that concerned him. He'd faced death so many times since this started that he'd come to feel it was a given he wouldn't live to be an old man. It wasn't Alistair's death, either. They were men of war, and each had made decisions to either start wars or remain in them. Death was part of that business.

Ares, without voicing it, had come to believe they might have their vengeance. That the Commonwealth and the damned Imperial Ascendant would fall.

Yet, all of this has been for nothing; that was what the little rolling machine was telling him. The whole thing would end either by a catastrophic event or the AllSeer's engineering.

He didn't lift his head as he asked, "Are you saying it's over?"

"I'm programmed to get you to Earth. I won't terminate that mission until you're dead or the algorithm is removed from your brain. I can't. No, it's not over. Not for you or me."

Ares didn't ask any other questions. The machine didn't have to give him any other answers. If Alistair died, the rebellion died, and their chances of getting away from the AllSeer were nearly zero.

Ares shook his head on his arm and chuckled despondently. How had everything ended up in Alistair's hands? Why couldn't the fate of mankind be dispersed through multiple people?

Alistair, you've got to figure something out, you big bastard, Ares thought. *Wherever you are, whatever you're doing, you've got to figure a way out of it. Otherwise? The rest of us are fucked.*

CHAPTER NINE

Alistair couldn't hear the sentiments being sent to him from across galaxies. He hadn't thought of Ares since he'd seen him get on a ship. He didn't know what had happened to his council or how many days had passed since he got to this black world.

The stranger had left him the small lamp, which allowed him to see a meter or so around him, but that was it. If he turned it off, it didn't matter whether his eyes were open or closed. All he saw was blackness.

Something had changed this morning, though, and it'd been growing stronger as the hours progressed. Most of the time, Alistair had done as the AllMother had taught him: worked on using his mind to break free of the constraints on him. He'd failed time after time; so far, no amount of concentration could shatter these aliens' abilities. He could only move mentally as far as they'd let him, and that was only within the room he occupied.

If Alistair had to guess, he'd say two days had passed since he awoke here. He didn't know how long he'd been unconscious while they patched him up. However, that put him at about twelve days of life left, and he was making no progress on saving himself.

Giving up wasn't an option, not only because of Luna but because of the insurrection. He'd keep trying to find his way out of this black prison until the black hole crushed them all.

Yet, when he woke up this morning, something was very different.

He hadn't done what he normally did, which was sit on his bed and concentrate. Instead, he'd remained lying down and tried to understand what he was feeling.

Hours had passed like that. Food was left at his door at certain intervals (to call anything morning here would make no sense). Alistair didn't rise to get it today, though. He remained in bed, letting this familiar feeling grow.

What was it?

Finally, he understood, and when he did, he shot out of bed and onto his feet. He felt for the lamp, grabbed the handle, and let the small light shine around him. He made his way to the door and banged on it. The aliens didn't let him move around as he pleased, but they were always watching and listening. They knew when he wanted something, and right now, he wanted this as much as anything ever.

"Open the godsdamn door!" he shouted as he banged on it. He didn't feel any pain in his hand despite hitting the surface as if it were an enemy. Adrenaline rushed through him and anger filled his mind. "Open it now!"

The door slowly slid into the wall and Alistair thrust the lamp forward, finding the shrouded stranger standing in front of him. "How long? How long have you had him?"

"He came with you. He crossed through the portal at the same time."

"Why didn't you fucking tell me?" Alistair wanted to grab the creature and pummel it to death. Only the knowledge that he couldn't do anything to it kept him at bay. He didn't know the limits of their mental power, only that it was stronger than his by orders of magnitude.

"We weren't sure what the creature was. We'd never seen anything like it. We wanted to look at it and understand better."

"Where's Obs?" Alistair said. "Did you hurt him?"

That had been the feeling growing in his body. It'd been the drathe, and whatever mental magic the aliens had practiced to keep Alistair from feeling it in the beginning, they'd relented. Now he felt him fully, and despite his question, Obs felt fine.

"Of course not," the alien said with disdain in his voice. "We are not animals. All creatures were made by the gods, whether they walk on four legs like that one or two like you."

"Where is he?"

The little creature cocked his head to the right. "That was my guess, that there was a bond between the two of you. There is, isn't there? Something was coming from the animal, but we didn't know what, so we blocked it. Today we decided to slowly release the block, but that's what it was this whole time—the animal's connection to you."

Alistair nearly growled. "Where is he?"

The stranger looked to his left, then Alistair heard the

DAVID BEERS & MICHAEL ANDERLE

drathe. Obs' huge feet bounded down the hallway, allowing him to move out of this creature's mental hold.

He stepped into the hallway, easily able to knock the alien over. Alistair didn't care who he hit.

The stranger moved out of the way, and Alistair saw Obs as he leaped into the light's circumference. The giant drathe had his paws up, jaw open and tongue lolling out of his mouth.

He hit Alistair with his full weight and the former Titan fell, unable to stay on his feet. He landed on his back and the lamp went skittering down the hallway, turning off as it disconnected from his hand.

Alistair couldn't see anything. He could only feel Obs' tongue lapping his face. Rough and wet, it brought tears to Alistair's face.

"Okay, okay, boy. Calm down. Calm down. Get off me."

The drathe wouldn't stop. After two minutes, Alistair grabbed him by his scruff and tossed him gently off, then hopped to his feet before the animal could restart the process.

He couldn't see a thing in the hallway but felt Obs move to his side. The animal leaned against him, both letting him know his presence was there and also seeming to gather strength from Alistair.

"Obs, find the lamp," Alistair said into the darkness. The drathe didn't move for a second, as if he was nervous stepping away might lose him Alistair yet again. "Go on. Get it for me."

The animal moved swiftly away, and Alistair heard him sniffing. Moments later, he felt the lamp being pushed into his hand. The hallway lit up again, and Alistair saw the stranger standing at the very edge of its glow.

"I knew it understood us," the alien whispered. "I've never heard of a beast that can understand language. What is it between you? Please tell me. When we dropped our blocks, how did you know it was him?"

For the first time since Alistair had spoken to the alien, he heard wonder in its voice.

"The drathe bonds with one person for life. He and I are soul-bonded, I guess is what you would call it. If I die, he'll die. I usually have a pretty good sense of where he is, at least when we're on the same planet. In the silence and darkness of this place, I guess I felt it stronger when you finally let us connect. It was the only familiar thing I could feel."

The stranger looked straight ahead, unable to see anything, but there was awe on his face. "Come with me," he whispered, then turned away from the two.

Alistair didn't move. He squatted next to Obs, put his arm around the beast, and leaned close to his ear. "We can't attack them, but we have to find a way off this planet. Stay next to me at all times. Don't leave my side unless I tell you."

He kissed the animal's head, then stood. The stranger was far up the hall and out of sight. Alistair walked fast, with Obs right at his side. The animal kept his nose to the ground, his sense of smell able to maneuver him much better in this environment.

In short order, they caught up with the stranger. He didn't turn around to look at either of them, and Alistair didn't venture out with his mind. For the first time since he'd opened his eyes in this place, he felt hope. He and Obs had conquered literal worlds, and they hadn't faced blind monks either.

Perhaps they'd survive this after all.

The stranger stepped onto an elevator Alistair hadn't known existed. The door closed, and while the alien remained still, the elevator began to rise.

"I want to show you our star," he said. "It is beautiful."

Alistair didn't respond, just remained standing next to his animal, wishing he had his Whip. He'd cut this damned planet apart if he had that, but he couldn't send Obs out looking for it, not with the abilities these creatures possessed.

The elevator came to a stop, and the stranger led them down another hallway. They twisted and turned through the labyrinth, but Alistair could tell they were on an incline. Moving closer to the planet's surface.

Finally, they reached a room, and it was the first light Alistair had seen beside his lamp since arriving.

They were at the surface, or as close to it as these aliens dared venture. Alistair didn't understand much about black holes or stars, but he understood radiation. The room they stood in should have been just as dark as the hallway outside, but the light coming from the far wall couldn't be contained.

Whatever was outside that wall was trying to get in and succeeding. Alistair had to squint and cover his face. He set the lamp on the first table he saw, and Obs turned his body and head away from the wall.

"I'll give your eyes a minute to adjust," the alien said, now standing behind them.

It took longer than a minute, but slowly Alistair's eyes did adjust to the room.

"You can't look at it full-on," the stranger told them. "This wall can give you percentages of its total brightness, but anything above eleven percent would permanently blind you. I won't bring it above two percent, but that'll be enough to let you see. Are you ready?"

Alistair looked at Obs, who was staring at the opposite wall. He wanted nothing to do with what these crazed two-legged creatures were up to.

"I'm ready," Alistair told the stranger.

The creature said nothing, but the black wall in front of him disappeared, and brilliant light such as Alistair had never seen burst through. Yellow, oranges, reds, blues, whites, all of them stretching out in a halo, obliterating his ability to see anything else.

He stepped closer to the wall, squinting but unable to keep from looking at something so beautiful.

He felt as if he were right next to the star. Like, if he were to walk out of this room and a hundred yards farther, he'd fall right into it.

Slowly, the black wall began to reclaim its space. The light dimmed until it looked like dusk. Alistair didn't turn to the alien. "It's miraculous."

"The gods understand beauty better than any of us," the creature whispered. "They understand life and death better than anyone who ever lived. They give us life, then they take it away. What you just saw is the end of the star burning out. Its fuel is almost gone. You've heard of a supernova, yes?"

Alistair nodded, his eyes adjusting to the new dimness.

"Our star isn't large enough to turn into one. Rather, it's going to collapse in on itself, bringing the other two planets in this star system as well as ours with it. The gravity will be so great, even light can't escape it. In its own way, it's just as beautiful as the star outside."

"The radiation alone…how isn't it killing you?"

"It's killed some of us. Our defenses are failing, and my body is beginning to burn because of the radiation that's breaking through. I can see that star with my mind and my mind alone. I don't have your eyes or any other way to view it. In the beginning, the gods did give us eyes, but that was so long ago that it's nearly been written out of our history. As our star expanded and the radiation grew worse, we were forced beneath the ground, and while our vision died, our psychic abilities came to life. I don't have eyes, but I don't need them."

"What do I look like to you?" Alistair said. "What do you see when you look at me?"

"Everything. Your shape. I can see the tiny way your chest moves as your heart beats beneath it. I can see the goosebumps on your skin when you're cold, and I can see your jaw tense when you're angry. Color is the only thing that might be different for us, but I can still see the sun's beautiful rays, and that's most important to me."

Alistair asked, "Why do you keep me here? I didn't mean to come, and neither did my animal. This was a mistake. I'm meant to be somewhere else, and so is he."

"I'm afraid the gods don't make mistakes. You were sent here, just as I was, and my species lives our lives on the basis of accepting. We have accepted it is our time to go."

Alistair turned and looked at the eyeless alien. "What if I wasn't sent here to die but to be saved?"

Obs trotted to his side again, sitting next to him and facing away from the shining wall.

"You know about humans," Alistair continued, "but how much do you know about what is happening right now?"

"Nothing." The alien said it without malice but without care. "We live lives of quiet contemplation. We focus on the gods and their will as they slowly show it to us."

Alistair nodded. On Earth, and probably other planets, there were people like this. Of course, on Earth, those who studied and worshipped the gods like these aliens were tiny religious sects whom everyone viewed suspiciously. Yet, he knew of them. "I promise you, I wasn't supposed to end up here. I had lost a war. I was being brought back to Earth, to humanity's home, to face trial and certain death. I was unconscious, so I can't say for certain what happened, but there isn't any way the Commonwealth sent me here. Nor could my people because they don't know this place exists."

He paused, staring at the alien, and understanding came over him. He couldn't be certain about anything, but what made sense was that someone had stepped in and sent him here. Otherwise, he'd be on Earth, or at least in the Solar System.

"You and your people need to consider that the will of the gods might not be that I die here. You need to consider that the gods sent me here to keep me from dying."

The stranger was quiet for a long time. Alistair said nothing. Obs sat at his side. The alien was considering something, and Alistair could only hope it was his words.

Finally, he said, "The chance is small that we have misunderstood the gods' desires, but it's possible. Maybe you and your animal aren't meant to die, but that isn't for me to say. It's a much larger conversation that you won't have a place in. You'll go back to your room with your animal, and I'll come to you with a decision when one is made."

Alistair did his best to control his emotions, but a sigh of relief escaped. Outside of seeing Obs, this was the best news he'd heard in a long time.

Inside his mind, he heard Prometheus chuckling. *It's not good news. They'll talk about letting us live.*

CHAPTER TEN

Dominik de Febian finished speaking to the Imperial Ascendant and stepped out of the box that allowed communication to take place. He rarely used it, though it had been in his family since his great-great-great-grandfather had taken over Neptune as Imperial Propraetor.

Neptune was four billion kilometers from Earth, and during Dominik's life, the Imperial Ascendant had never made his way out here. Dominik had only been to Earth a few times, the last being when Alexander had called all the propraetors to the homeworld.

Dominik, as well as Neptune, stayed out of the Commonwealth's affairs. Out here on the Edge planets, life was different from those near the sun. It was harder. Dominik was harder. The de Febians all saw themselves as harder.

The discussion with the Ascendant hadn't been what Dominik had hoped, but it had been what he'd expected. The insurrection would of course start on Neptune now that Pluto was a dead planet. Going to Earth to fight first wouldn't make sense since that would rally people unlike anything else. An attack on the Commonwealth's home-world was unthinkable for most.

Dominik understood that Kane wasn't with the insurrection, though he wasn't sure how he felt about the man. The threat was real; Dominik didn't doubt that. The current Imperial Ascendant didn't move from his throne without a reason, and this was the most movement Dominik had ever seen from him.

As far as propraetors went, Dominik was relatively young. He was in his mid-forties, about Kane's age, and during his reign, Neptune had done well. The average life span had increased to just over one hundred, an increase of ten years. Finita-189 mining had increased fifteen percent, and despite that, Neptune had begun replenishing its diminished supply of the chemical.

Dominik rarely thought about where he would be ranked among great Neptune propraetors. He focused on day-to-day affairs and making sure Neptunians' lives were improving.

He was a peace-time propraetor. At least, he had been.

Now, war was coming to his planet, and he knew he would have to change. The coming war could burn everything he and his forebears had built to the ground.

Dominik left the box and went to find his wife.

It was early afternoon on Neptune, and she was at her desk as usual at this time. Like Dominik, Ona de Febian was short and sturdily built. Those born on Neptune faced a stronger gravity than the people of Earth, which meant stronger muscles and tendons but shorter bodies. In a hand-to-hand fight, most Neptunians would easily overpower their brothers and sisters from smaller planets.

Neptune had been what was once called an icy gas giant until the terraforming changed everything. Finita-189's energy source had made it feasible to do, and the large supply on and around Neptune gave humanity the desire to undertake such a tremendous task. Without that fuel, Neptune would still be an icy gas giant instead of Dominik's home. It would never have the classic beauty of Earth since its distance from the sun didn't allow for the same flora. Even terraforming couldn't warm the planet to Earthlike temperatures, though life did survive. The winds of old still existed, and they weren't anything you wanted to get caught up in without protective gear. Even the youngest Neptunian knew that.

To live on Neptune, strength was a must for both men and women. That strength led to pride, and every propraetor's wife since the first had taken an active role in ruling the massive planet.

Ona looked up from her desk. The top of it was a large DataTrack, and as Dominik dropped his eyes to it, he saw she was looking at troop numbers. She was already preparing for war, despite waiting to hear from him.

"What did he tell you?"

Dominik nodded. "It's war. The Subversives' plan isn't bad. They're sending the mercenaries in their fleet through the fifth dimension while the rest wait at the portal. It'll be a simultaneous attack at the portal and from above."

Ona looked back at the DataTrack. He doubted his wife had even wondered what he would say next. Neptunians didn't look outside for assistance.

"Most of the fleet that went to Phoenix was Mars- and Mercury-made. The Ascendant made sure his Earth fleet was safe, though he did use quite a few of his Titans. He's sending us assistance from Saturn and Uranus, as well as the Martians. He said he's going to keep his Titans on Earth for now but will send assistance if it's needed."

Ona glanced up with narrowed eyes. "Did you accept the assistance?"

Dominik wanted to smile, but he knew better than to do so. His wife didn't want assistance. Neptune would defend Neptune. "Of course. When our liege commands something, we do as he says."

She continued looking at him for a second, her disapproval obvious. She wasn't going to challenge him, though, not because she *wouldn't* challenge her husband, but because she knew in this instance he was correct. Finally, she changed the subject. "Have you seen the mercenary they sent?"

"I was heading there next."

During the battle on Phoenix, one of the mercenaries had tried to save Kane, but in doing so had ended up on Earth. He could travel in the fifth dimension, so he'd been shipped to Neptune so Dominik could get a look at what the creatures were like. He'd never heard of them before, the gigantes.

They were supposedly ferocious fighters.

"We've got a few more days before they arrive," Ona said, "according to the latest reports. We'll need to discuss strategy shortly. I've got most of it worked out, but I want you to look it over."

"Of course," Dominik responded. "I should be free in a few hours. I'll find you here?"

His wife nodded.

"You'll see the number of troops and aircraft the Ascendant is sending shortly if it's not already on your Data-Track." He knew his wife didn't want to put them into her calculations or strategy, and he raised an eyebrow. "When I come back, they'll be included, right?"

"I'm no fool, Dominik. We'll use them as commanded."

"Thank you." He walked to the other side of the desk and kissed her cheek. "I'll see you shortly."

Exiting the room, Dominik's thoughts went to the beast he was going to view. He'd had time to read up on them. They were creatures bred for nothing but war, going through trial after trial until they 'graduated,' which meant they were given to the highest bidder.

It was an odd thing that Dominik couldn't wrap his mind around. These creatures were taught to serve the strongest, and if a buyer wasn't stronger than their rival, the creature would switch sides. They held loyalty only to strength, but apparently, they were stronger than any of the buyers who took them off their homeworld.

Dominik understood following strength, but he didn't understand changing allegiance.

Yet, this Kane man had changed all of that for them. He'd conquered their world and freed them after. Now they followed him of their own volition. The truth was that Kane couldn't be found, yet they were heading to Neptune. They were continuing his war without him.

The creature was being held in solitude beneath the ground. Dominik had made sure the mercenary was close because he didn't want to waste time traveling. Beneath the propraetor's residence was a prison that had been used a lot in previous regimes. Even during his, it'd been used back when the Subversives were a problem. Since they'd left, the prison had been empty.

Until now.

The elevator took Dominik to the bottom level. The prison was the same as the rest of Neptune: hard. The floors were stone, the walls as well. Only the barriers separating the prisoners from the guards were more advanced. Dominik had made them DataTracks, yet impenetrable. Prisoners could pull up anything on their side of the transparent barrier, allowing them to look up information and speak to others. Really, they could do anything they wanted.

He reached the cell that held the prisoner.

The creature sat on the floor opposite him. His knees were up and his forearms rested on them. He had a human look to him, but Dominik immediately knew he'd not come from a woman's womb.

The gigante stood at the sight of Dominik, and that was when the propraetor understood his true size. He had to duck inside the cell since no Neptunian had ever thought they would cage something so tall. One of his hands was like two of Dominik's. The gigante's leg was the size of Dominik's entire torso.

The thing approached the barrier but didn't touch it. Dominik stared into his eyes, and he didn't find a dull beast looking back at him. Intelligence was inside this creature.

"Do you have a name?" Dominik asked.

"Caesar," the beast answered, his voice the deepest Dominik had ever heard.

"Do you know who I am?"

Caesar shook his head.

"Do you know where you are?"

Another no.

"You are on Neptune, and I'm its ruler. Do you know about Neptune? Of the Commonwealth's Solar System?"

The creature nodded. Dominik couldn't tell if he was lying, but there wasn't any reason for him to, not after his previous answers.

"How many are there like you, Caesar? How many gigantes?"

The ducking giant smirked, his big lips parting to reveal huge white teeth. "I am the only one."

It was the first time Dominik had heard him say a sentence, and his language was somewhat stilted, a bit formal. It wasn't the first language he'd learned to speak.

"I'm afraid you're lying to me, given that there's an entire fleet of creatures just like you coming to attack my world. I'm curious how many are there. You're not going to tell me, though, right?"

"I just did. I'm the only one," the gigante said, still wearing that smirk.

Dominik wasn't a leader who used torture as a weapon. It was beneath him. Yet, to learn about this creature and perhaps the others who were coming, he wanted to test something.

"The man you follow; they call him Prometheus. He's gone. He's not coming with the rest of your kind, and he's not with the humans waiting to cross through the portal. I won't lie to you because you're never leaving this cell. No one knows where he is, but when your insurrection attacks my planet, he won't be with them."

The smirk faded from the giant's face. Dominik couldn't read what was in the thing's eyes. Maybe sadness, maybe not.

"He went through the portal. I believe you saw that happen, but he didn't return to Earth like you did. He went somewhere else, and no one knows where."

The beast turned away from Dominik and walked to the other side of the room. He sat as he had before, not saying anything.

Dominik wasn't done yet. He'd seen the sheer massiveness of the creature, which was something to worry about in the coming battle. He wanted to know more about his psyche, though. "Prometheus freed you, didn't he? He freed all of your kind?"

Caesar blinked but remained silent.

"Is he the strongest you've seen? Is that why you follow him, or is there some other reason?"

The gigante stared past Dominik, looking at the rest of the prison, a place he would never touch.

"If you won't answer those questions, will you answer this one?"

The prisoner turned his eyes to the ruler.

"If Kane wasn't leading you, if he was lost or even dead, would you have come here? Would you have continued your insurrection?"

The gigante gave him that lazy blink again as if nothing in the world mattered except a long nap.

"Prometheus is not lost. He is not dead. The likes of you and your ilk cannot kill him. I'll answer your questions. Yes, he freed me, and then he went and freed my brothers. He's the strongest creature I've ever seen, including the one in front of me now. If he were dead, I would fight his war until my heart stopped beating. He is not dead, though, and when he gets here in all his furious glory, you're going to wish you'd never heard the *myth* of Prometheus, let alone of the real man."

Caesar was alone again.

It'd been quite a ride to get here, only to remain in one place without moving. He'd slid through the portal and found himself staring at a host of Commonwealth soldiers. He'd fought as well as he could, but there were just too many. They hadn't killed him, probably because they hadn't known what he was. They wanted to know more about him.

Days passed and they made Caesar whole again, patching up his wounds. He, of course, could have healed himself, but he didn't want to give them any information about his species.

At some point, they'd put him aboard a transport with another mutant, and they'd made it to this planet.

Since then, it'd been boredom and waiting. They'd told him nothing.

The meeting with the short man was the first information he'd received. Prometheus was lost? Caesar didn't believe it. It was not that he couldn't; he simply didn't.

Perhaps the man was lying, but Caesar had sensed no deception in him.

Prometheus hadn't been on the other side of the portal when Caesar crashed through, but he *had* been tossed through right before. Caesar remembered Obs crossing at the same time. It was he who'd been last.

Where was Prometheus? He wasn't with the council or the insurrection.

They were coming, though. Thoreaux was going forward without Prometheus. He would go forward if he was the only one left, just like Prometheus.

War is coming, he thought. *I must get out of here. Somehow. I cannot let my brothers fight alone.*

Staring into the stone prison, he saw no way to escape.

He told himself one thing, and it was the *only* thing that gave him any hope.

Prometheus wasn't dead, and as long as he lived, they had a chance.

Dominik allowed himself alcohol in the rarest of moments. Many people, including Neptunians, drank to celebrate. Dominik didn't. In the good times, he wanted to remember them without the haze of intoxicants. Many people drank in the depths of despair, but Dominik found them weak. At no time in the history of mankind had intoxicants helped pull someone out of whatever issue threatened to destroy them. No, intoxicants only hastened the demise.

Dominik drank when a problem presented itself, one he couldn't immediately solve. He didn't drink to excess since that would be as helpful as a man drinking in despair. He sipped whiskey, the kind made on his planet, and he thought. Alcohol allowed his usual hard, logical mind to open up a bit. He could free himself from the normal constraints he imposed on it.

He preferred to do it outside on one of many of his terraces.

The sun was descending below the horizon. He'd seen the sunset on Earth, and he preferred Neptune's. Earth's might have brighter hues that scattered farther, but here on Neptune, one could stare at it without risking blindness.

The terraforming had created a very heavy atmosphere that kept the little heat that reached them within the planet's grasp. Still, it was cold, and as night fell, it grew colder.

Dominik put a jacket around his shoulders. His chair faced the terrace's railing.

He heard his wife step outside and the door close behind her.

She stopped beside his chair. He'd pulled one up for her, but she didn't sit. Rather, she placed her hands on the back of it and looked at the sunset. "The prisoner unnerved you?"

"I'm not sure I'd put it that way, but yes, he made me want to consider some things."

Ona went around to the front of the chair and sat. She moved her open right hand toward him, signaling that she wanted a sip. Dominik handed it to her, and she drank shallowly before handing the glass back.

"What is it you're considering?" she asked after she swallowed.

"Men aren't made to fight such creatures. Giants are

going to land on Neptune. Creatures bigger than any of us have imagined except maybe in the tales we were told as children."

"What else?" Ona said.

He took a sip of his whiskey, thinking he loved his wife. He wouldn't be out here just because of that, and she knew it. "He speaks of that Titan as if he were a god. I wanted to see the creature's reaction when I told him his leader was lost. His response was resolution. He said the man wasn't lost, that he'd get here, and then Neptune wouldn't exist any longer."

"It's a ghost my husband considers," Ona mused. "Have you come up with how you'll deal with this ghost?"

Dominik frowned. "No, but I can consider that later. We've got a few more days before those giants are going to fill our skies. Reinforcements will start arriving tomorrow. What's my wife's plan?"

CHAPTER ELEVEN

The war was almost upon Thoreaux, mere days away, and he hadn't stopped questioning himself since the gigantes left in the fleet.

There'd been no news from or about Prometheus, which frightened Thoreaux more with each passing day. If Prometheus could get in touch with them, he would have, and if he could have reached them, he'd already be here.

Neither had happened.

Thoreaux was in charge, and Servia was his second in command. Each knew they weren't equipped for what was coming, and without saying it to one another, each secretly prayed Prometheus would show up.

Thoreaux sat with Servia now inside a small Terram room. Red rock surrounded them, and the chairs and table they were using were built out of it.

Servia had the Neptune portal schematics pulled up on a DataTrack and a holovid floating between the two of them. "The good thing about this portal is its size. Due to Neptune's sheer mass, it needed to be bigger and stronger than any portal we've ever encountered. Also, it's above ground, which gives us more options, rather than the one we'll be streaming through here on Phoenix."

Using her fingertips, she zoomed out, the holovid showing a large portion of the planet. The portal looked smaller from this view, but Thoreaux could see its size relative to other portals.

Watching the holovid, Servia continued her update. "Because of the Commonwealth's secrecy regarding their portals and usage, this part of the planet is largely uninhabited, which creates some advantages for us. I've got no idea why they say people can't live there, but that doesn't matter to us right now. I imagine soon, Neptunians will know they've been lied to, and that's something that helps us if we win. We can use it against the Commonwealth."

Thoreaux's eyes were narrowed. "Long way to go before that, though."

"Yup," Servia agreed. "I've talked to Jeeves, and there are two ways we can go about flowing through the portal. We can put us all on one side, or he can alternate side to side so we're split up until he shuts down the portal. When it's not operational anymore, one group will be able to watch the other's six."

She looked through the holovid at Thoreaux.

"If they have all their forces on one side of the portal, that could create some disadvantages. If they're circling the portal, having people on both sides helps us. I wanted to run it by you and see what you think."

Thoreaux nodded, understanding the predicament. "If we come out on one side and they've got the thing surrounded, none of their weapons will be able to hit us until the portal is dormant, right?"

"Not sure," Servia answered. She glanced at the Data-Track. "Jeeves, you hear that question?"

"Yes, madam," he said in his odd accent. "That is true. As long as the portal is active, nothing fired through the arch will reach the other side. Lasers aren't going to make it through either since the black hole concepts the tech is based on say weapons can't fire through. It keeps someone on another planet from attacking across the universe."

Thoreaux liked the sound of that. It was the best thing he'd heard the past week. "Now the question is, how long can you keep control of the portal, Jeeves. If you can hold it for an hour, we've cut off half of Neptune's force, at least until they circle back around. What's the perimeter of that thing?"

Jeeves took the last question first. "It might be easier for me to put it in terms of human movement. For an average man with a MechSuit, it would take them about an hour to walk from one side of the portal to the other. Movement around it will be arduous, especially for a large number of people."

The AI paused for a second. "I've been studying how the Commonwealth is using the portal since we took control of the planet. The AI program they're using isn't compli-cated, which helps them in this instance. It was built primarily for portal control, and that specialization allows it much greater versatility. I cannot hold the portal for an hour. It will break through before that."

"Well," Thoreaux said, "what are you thinking? How long?"

"The calculations here are based on us getting our troops through, but at a distance that allows us not to topple over one another. I cannot stress how important that is, Thoreaux. If the Terram and humans trip over one another, we've got no chance." The AI paused as if to emphasize it. Thoreaux understood that. He and Servia had used Jeeves' calculations to figure out how quickly each group should run through.

Jeeves continued. "To get everyone through, it's going to take a half an hour, and that's cutting it close. Some might not make it across. I think I can hold the AI off for that much time, but no longer. It might get through my defenses at twenty-five minutes."

Thoreaux nodded and leaned back. He wanted to pace but knew he couldn't. He needed to be able to study what came up on the DataTrack. "We've got to figure out the AllMother problem. We can't leave her here. The AllSeer would reemerge within hours, I imagine, and that would be the end of her. She obviously can't go through with the first groups, and I don't want to wait until the last in case the Commonwealth takes control of the portal again. That means middle groups." He tilted his head up to find Servia. "What do we do then? She'll be sitting on a battlefield defenseless."

"I've been thinking about that," Servia said. She zoomed in on the portal. "We've kept most of the de Monaham hybrids back with us. Aspen isn't going to be much help out there either. This is what I say we do to make sure the AllMother isn't killed or captured." She zoomed in to the far left side of the portal. "We use Relm, fifty hybrids, and the banshees—"

"The what?" Thoreaux interrupted.

"That's what Relm's taken to calling the women Aspen trusts the most. They're dangerous, and Relm's been practicing non-stop with the gloves they use. Anyway, we use them to form a protective circle around the AllMother and Aspen. We'll put tracking devices on those two, and the fleet above will drop a transport with two corvettes. The transport picks up those two, and the corvettes fight off anything that tries to attack it as it gets back to the fleet above."

The holovid showed the ships dropping to the planet, then heading right back up into the sky. Servia shrugged as she turned her attention back to Thoreaux. "I can't think of a better way to do it. It's not perfect, but nothing in this is. What do you think?"

"Did you run it by Mother yet?"

Servia shook her head. "Wanted to get your approval first. She's outta fuel, though, and she knows it. She won't be able to do anything on that planet. Plus, the winds on Neptune could toss her a kilometer if one of those storms hits. She'll go along with the plan."

"Aspen? Have you talked to him?"

"Yes," Servia answered with a nod. "He's not happy about it. He doesn't want to let his warriors fight without him. The kid's changed a good bit since he went to war last, but he relented in the end. He knows he'd just be a liability."

"All right." Thoreaux glanced at the DataTrack. "Jeeves, anything here we are missing with that plan? Or does it compute? Do you have any odds that the AllMother makes it to the fleet safely?"

"There are four hundred and thirty-two things wrong with the plan, but anything else has more issues. It's the best we have. They're most likely moving many of their land-to-air defenses to cover the area surrounding the portal, so that's going to make it a lot harder to get the transport to the ground and back up. That said, I put the odds of her survival at forty-seven percent. We just have to use the fleet to protect her as well as the corvettes."

There were so many things to consider. To Thoreaux, they seemed endless, and as he planned this battle, his respect for Prometheus grew. Thoreaux had imagined the pressure his leader had been under all those times, but he hadn't experienced it. Now he was in the midst of it, and it nearly overwhelmed him every second of every day. Remembering that Pro had handled it was the only thing that kept him steady.

"That brings us to the next issue," he said. "I want Faitrin with those two, and I want her in that transport going back to the fleet. She can fight, but her tactical advantage is going to be piloting the fleet, so the transport is bringing all three back up there."

He paused. He'd thought long and hard about the next issue.

"The gigantes. They contribute almost nothing by being up there. They can't harmonize with ships, and even though they're flying them right now, they aren't trained for that type of battle. We need them here, and we need the pilots up there." He had told Servia about this issue before and only recapped so everyone listening now knew about it. "Serv, have you figured that out?"

Servia smiled. It was the one she'd given Pro back on

Pluto when Thoreaux hadn't trusted the man but she'd believed in him. "Yeah, I've got a plan, but you're not going to like it."

Thoreaux rubbed both of his hands through his hair. "Let me hear it."

The AllMother hadn't spoken to anyone in days. She trusted Prometheus' generals to figure out the best plan of attack and knew she had nothing to add.

She remained in the small room the Terram had given her, only venturing out for food. No one had come to her, either, and she didn't know if that was a good or bad sign.

The AllMother rarely questioned her decisions. When one lived to be over a thousand years old, one had seen most things more than once. Now, though, alone in her room made of rock, she wondered if she'd made the right decision when they'd been freeing the gigante. She'd used herself up, thinking it was necessary for survival.

It probably had been, but now she was almost empty. When she was younger, the well that was filled with gifts had replenished itself so quickly, she hardly ever noticed when the water level dropped.

Now the well was there, but the water barely trickled in. She had been able to refill some, but nothing that would matter in the coming battle. On Neptune, she'd be useless to Thoreaux, and he had to know that.

As she sat alone, she mused about where her protege had gone. None of the others in the council had the time to wonder *how* that had happened. That was what the

AllMother wanted to know. Prometheus should have ended up in the Solar System, but someone had intervened. Someone had put him elsewhere, and she didn't think it was her brother.

Whatever power the AllSeer possessed, it didn't extend to controlling a universe's technology.

Someone else had done it, and the AllMother couldn't fathom who.

She didn't think Prometheus was dead, only removed from the battlefield, and she wasn't sure her well was full enough to allow her mind to venture off this planet, let alone search galaxies for him.

Everyone had to know they were doomed on Neptune if they didn't find him. They could make all the best plans, but the AllMother had waited centuries for Pro because she knew what was needed: a champion.

The well refilled slowly, but there was something in there now. Using it wouldn't matter, at least not for the coming battle. She needed to send him a message. Perhaps he could use his well to find it.

The AllMother didn't know if it was possible, only that Prometheus had to hear about the coming danger. She didn't doubt he was doing everything in his power to return to them, but if he heard about the urgency, perhaps his miraculous mind would figure something out.

The AllMother sat on the edge of her cot, her feet touching the rock floor.

She reached into the well and did something she'd never done before. It was like the message-in-a-bottle stories she'd heard as a kid, when stranded people would cast something into the ocean, hoping it would make land some-where. More often than not, those bottles returned to the island they were sent from, but that was all she could do.

The AllMother didn't try to force her mind anywhere; she simply sent a message. She didn't follow it or send it in any one direction. Hopefully, it would spread out like a gaseous cloud, but she didn't have enough power to direct it like that.

Prometheus, get to Neptune. We need you.

That was it, and when it left her mind, the well was empty again. It would be months before she could do something even that meager again.

She sighed, staring at her feet.

The sound of someone walking outside her room filtered to her ears, and she looked up.

Thoreaux came through the doorway, and the AllMother sat up.

"You don't look well, Mother."

"I promise, you've looked better too, my son," she said with a wry smile. "Is there news?"

He stepped farther into the room and immediately started the pacing she knew so well. She found it oddly comforting, even though he only did it when he was thinking seriously about a problem he couldn't solve.

"We've got plans to help you survive this," he told her, "but they aren't great. It's a forty-seven-percent chance of survival."

"I've faced much worse than that." Her voice was calm because he needed it to be. "You know I trust your deci-sions as I do Pro's. Whatever you tell me to do, I'll do it."

He reached the far end of her room and turned. "Have you heard from him?"

There wasn't any need to ask who 'him' was. "No. I don't think I could hear from him if I wanted to."

Thoreaux stopped walking and peered at his feet. "Do you think he's alive? If he's not, all of this should stop now. I'm only sending countless numbers of people to die if he's gone." He nodded, but it was to himself. "If Pro's dead, this ends. I haven't said that to anyone else, but that is my decision. I won't kill so many for no reason."

He met her eyes. "I'm sorry if that goes against everything you've taught me or makes you change your idea of who I am, but that's the truth. If he's dead, so are we if we continue. I'm fine with my death, but not all the rest."

The AllMother smiled, and unbidden tears came to her eyes. She couldn't remember the last time she'd cried. It didn't matter if it happened now, so she didn't fight them. "Nothing would change my idea of you, Thoreaux. You're my son, just as your father was. In your position, I might even say the same thing you did. Prometheus is the reason I waited to face down the Commonwealth in full force. Your assessment is right. If he's dead, so is everyone else."

She paused, still smiling, as a single tear fell from her eye. She didn't wipe it away.

"I can't tell you if he's alive. I honestly don't know. I can only tell you what I believe, and it's the same thing I've always believed. He's the one I chose, and he's going to lead us to victory. I believe he's alive because to do that, he has to be. I could be wrong, Thoreaux. I could be blinded by my faith, but if you want my answer, that's it. He's out there, and he's coming back to us."

Thoreaux looked at his feet again. He was fighting back tears too, and she watched as he gritted his teeth, jaw flexing, pushing down the emotions that threatened to burst through his calm demeanor.

Once he had himself under control, he nodded again. "We'll go forward. We'll take Neptune. I've gotta go talk to Relm, but Servia is going to come and tell you our plan to get you off the planet." He looked up. "I love you, Mother."

"I love you too, son." She stood and walked over to him, placing one hand on his right shoulder. "For some, living by faith is an impossibility. They need cold, hard facts to show them which way to go. For me, living by faith makes this a lot easier. I don't need to worry about outside factors because my faith tells me we're going to make it. Right now, while you're in this position, I think you should blind yourself with your faith. Just know he's coming, and it's our job to have everything ready when he gets here."

Tears stood in his eyes again. "Okay, then. I'll do that, but I'm gonna kick his ass for taking so long when this is all over."

Servia hadn't asked Thoreaux certain questions, though she had to know the answers to them. When the AllMother's people had escaped Pluto, that hadn't been the only planet they resided on. The insurrection had people throughout the Solar System, including on Earth. The Commonwealth had spies everywhere, and the insurrection tried to do the same.

Neptune was no different. There were people on that

planet loyal to the AllMother, people who would die for her.

Servia hadn't asked what Thoreaux had heard from them, though she had to know he'd reached out over their channels. Thoreaux supposed it was because she trusted him to handle that information and tell her anything relevant. She had enough to do, given everything he'd charged her with.

Information had just come through, though, and it was more than important. That was why he had to talk to Relm.

It would change some of the plans regarding the AllMother's escape, but Thoreaux wasn't going to bring it up until he'd spoken to Relm about it.

He found the council member in the arena where Pro had killed one of the Myrmidons. That small battle felt like decades ago, though it had only been months.

Relm was practicing with one of the Monaham women. Thoreaux supposed it was one of the banshees, but right now, he didn't care. Relm was wearing the gloves and taking instructions on how to use them, but the practice stopped when they saw him enter.

"What's up, broth?" Relm called from the other side of the arena.

Thoreaux kept walking across the dusty ground, heading to them. "Need to talk to you, Relm. You got a minute?"

Relm took off the gloves and bowed to the woman. She walked toward the entrance, passing Thoreaux as she did. She gave him a curt nod but said nothing. She understood what Thoreaux meant: he needed to talk to Relm alone.

Thoreaux reached Relm, and the young man's eyebrows rose. "Don't tell me he's dead, broth. I can't take that right now."

Thoreaux shook his head. "No, no. Nothing like that. We haven't heard anything about Pro. This is different, and I haven't shared it with anyone else yet. What I'm going to tell you, you have to keep to yourself too. Got it?"

"Yeah, of course, broth. What's up?"

"One of our spies on Neptune got us some important information today." He met Relm's eyes, the emotion he'd felt with the AllMother gone. This was business. This could be life or death. "Caesar is on Neptune. He's being kept in a prison beneath the propraetor's residence."

Relm's eyes widened and his jaw dropped. No one had spoken much about Caesar since they'd lost him to the portal. Thoreaux felt guilty about it, but there wasn't anything that could be done. Plus, there were many more things they had to consider. Now, though, they had confirmation of where the gigante was, and Thoreaux couldn't ignore that.

"My first question is, why are you telling *me*?" Relm asked.

"Logically, it doesn't matter where he is," Thoreaux told him. "I know I shouldn't be telling anyone about this, but I made it known throughout our networks that if anyone saw Pro or Caesar, they should get word to me." Thoreaux turned and looked at the stands, into which the Terram had crowded to watch Pro fight that Myrmidon. "Logically, Caesar is just one gigante, and we have a host of them. I shouldn't worry about whether or not we've lost him. I certainly shouldn't consider trying to save him."

DAVID BEERS & MICHAEL ANDERLE

He stopped turning with his back to Relm.

"The scars that bitch gave me are gone—the ones on my body, at least. Hel was her name, and I'll never forget it. There wasn't any reason for Pro to come get me, but he did. He risked everything, including his life, to get me away from that psychopath."

Thoreaux nodded, confirming to himself what he was going to do. He glanced at Relm. "We're moving on Neptune very soon. The only job you have is to get Caesar out of that prison. You're going alone because I think that's our best chance of getting him out. Once we get there and the war starts, they aren't going to think about the prisoner they have beneath that fortress. That's how you'll be able to get him out. Will you do it?"

Relm gazed at the gloves in his right hand. "Yeah, Thoreaux. I'll do whatever you tell me to. If it's fighting at the portal or saving Caesar, it's all the same to me." He shook the gloves lightly. "I wonder, though, would you care if I brought Nero with me? He's the only gigante who didn't get on the ships, and I've talked to him about it over the past few days. He's a weird guy, Nero, but he said his purpose wasn't in the sky this time. I guess he meant back when Pro and he got caught up on the Ice Queen's dreadnought."

He shoved the gloves into his back pocket, then looked at Thoreaux.

"I don't know, Caesar said he was touched or something, but I'd feel safer if he was with me. You care if I take him?"

Thoreaux hadn't thought about Nero during the planning process. He honestly hadn't known the gigante had remained on Phoenix until just now. "No, go ahead. The two of you go get Caesar."

"All right, broth, we'll do it. No problem."

Thoreaux waited, expecting the question that everyone was asking everyone. Did he think Prometheus was alive?

But Relm said nothing. After a second, he asked, "What?"

"Figured you would ask something else about Pro is all. Seems like we all do it now. I just did with the AllMother."

Relm shook his head, turning his face to the stands. A weird smile curled his lips. "Nero talked about him a little bit."

Thoreaux stepped forward, raising his eyebrows. "Something useful?"

Relm gave a slight shake of his head. "I don't think so, or I would have brought it to you. I mean, you know how Nero is. Hell, Pro named him that because of that insane emperor back in Rome. He said he wasn't worried about Pro, and I shouldn't worry either. He said the time for worrying would come later, but it wasn't here yet." Relm looked at Thoreaux and shrugged. "That's it, but I believe the crazy giant. I was scared when you walked in here, but that was just the look on your face. I think Nero is right. The time for worry isn't here yet."

Thoreaux scratched his temple. "I wish I was as crazy as that giant. It'd be nice to have that sorta peace." He put his hand down. "We'll talk more in the next two days. We cross the portal in seventy-two hours."

CHAPTER TWELVE

Alistair stood in the middle of a dark room. Obs was at his side, as he had been since they'd reunited. Neither the human nor drathe would permit themselves to be separated on this planet again, not for even a moment. They would rather die than let that happen. However, the nameless aliens didn't attempt to keep them from one another.

No, Alistair and Obs were left together and left alone. Alistair had spent his time concentrating on escape and speaking to Obs.

The drathe had spent his time sleeping and listening to his master. Whether the animal thought they had a chance to escape or not was anyone's guess, but as long as he was by Alistair's side, he seemed to be at peace.

The stranger finally arrived, and given the darkness they lived in, Alistair couldn't say how much time had passed.

"Some of the others would like to speak with you," he said from beneath his cowl. "They aren't going to transform themselves into this shape as I have, and we all agree that our natural form is too much for you to handle, so there will be no lamp nor light for you."

"I promise you, the current form you inhabit isn't all that comforting, but as you wish," Alistair responded. "When do they want to see me?"

"Now. You're to follow me."

Alistair supposed that when life was nearly over for them, there wasn't any time for waiting. He made no argument but stood from the cot. Obs followed, and the three left the room.

The darkness in the hallways and elevators was complete, but the stranger allowed Alistair's mind to expand a bit farther. He was able to see the stranger, though not quite the same way the stranger had described seeing him. Alistair was able to follow, though, and Obs never once left his right leg.

The two of them stood in pitch-blackness now. The aliens had allowed Alistair's mind to expand even more, letting him see almost the entire room he stood in, though stopping his abilities just before he saw them. Alistair couldn't imagine what they looked like, but they were certainly not so hideous or otherworldly as to drive him insane just from a glance. Yet, they kept themselves hidden.

Alistair said nothing. He remained in the middle of the room, eyes closed, trying to see as the stranger told him he could.

The first voice that spoke came from in front of and above Alistair. It wasn't the voice of the alien who usually interacted with Alistair, but someone new.

"Do you believe in the gods?" the voice asked. It was a whisper that seemed to snake around the outer edge of the room before finding Alistair.

"I've never considered them," he responded. "I suppose I do believe in them, though whatever they are, I don't believe they care much about us."

Whisper-like chuckles came from wherever the creatures were. Alistair couldn't make out how many there were, not even with the different noises of laughter.

Eventually, their giggling died and another voice spoke. "If the gods told you to do something, even if it meant your death, would you do it?"

"Like you and this star?" he responded.

"Precisely."

"I would need to know without a doubt it was the gods speaking to me, not other voices in my head."

"What then?" the voice continued. "If you could be sure of who was commanding you, would you listen?"

Alistair was silent for a few moments, thinking about the question. He hadn't been brought before these aliens to give them platitudes. They'd know if he lied. Alistair didn't know what these creatures wanted; he couldn't figure that out, but they had to want *something*. Otherwise, none of them would be here. They were questioning their own beliefs about what the gods wanted.

Obs gently nuzzled his knee, letting him know he was taking too long to answer.

"I'd have to know the reason, even if I knew it was the gods who wanted me to do it."

No laughter came from above. No whispered asides.

The aliens were silent. That wasn't the answer they wanted. Perhaps they couldn't even understand it. Much the same as their true forms were so far out of Alistair's ability to view the physical world, maybe his answer had been too dissimilar philosophically.

"I was raised," he continued, "to believe a single man was the equivalent of the gods. My whole life, I looked at him as unquestionable. He was the beginning and the end for everyone within his purview. I did everything he asked without questioning his orders." He took a deep breath, allowing his mind to rest. He stopped trying to expand past the border the creatures had set up. "Until one time, I decided to go against what that man wanted, and since then, I've been hunted every day of my life. I can draw a line from that moment to this one, all because I didn't follow one order."

The question came as a whisper without a beat between his last word and the speaker's. "Did you make a mistake in disobeying? You stand before a strange species, blind, your only friend an animal. Would you take that choice back if you could, Alistair Kane?"

He nodded, but not in answer, only showing that he understood the question. He knelt as Obs moved in front of his knees, leaning on him as Alistair ran his hands through his pelt. In the room's darkness, Alistair didn't have to close his eyes to see Luna. His wife's face filled the blackness in front of him.

His next few words were whispered as he petted the drathe. "If I'd listened, I'd be with you right now, wouldn't I?"

The aliens above said nothing to his question, though he knew they'd heard it.

Alistair stood up, knowing his answer. "If I had to make the choice again, I would do the same thing. I wouldn't follow the order, and if it put me here, about to be crushed by a black hole, blind, and with Obs by my side, then so be it. I made the right choice."

A different voice spoke this time. It sounded as if it came from Alistair's right, and was older than the others. "You exemplify the issue our order has with your species. I know my brother has explained it to you, but your inability to accept the will of the gods or the universe or whatever you want to term it is, quite frankly, insane. The example you give us here shows that you are crazy. You'd rather die with us than live with your wife, rather than accept a being's order who was your superior, and are the gods not all our superiors?"

"An evil god is no more superior than an evil man."

The alien sighed. "I am out of time, and I have no desire to play word games with you, Alistair Kane. The reality is thus: we only have a few days before our planet can no longer handle the pull of our dying star, then our time here is done. By whatever way you got here, it is certainly a strange occurrence, and much debate about the will of the gods has taken place while we await our deaths. Some think their will is that you die with us, while others believe their will hasn't been told yet. For those who believe that, confining you to this dying world is unthinkable."

The voice paused for a few moments, but Alistair could hear the decision in the pause. Whoever spoke now, he held more authority than the others here, and certainly more than the stranger who had guided him along the hallways.

"In my long years, I've heard the Commonwealth's trite saying: 'One people, one purpose.'" He chuckled at the mantra, his laughter sounding like a dry leaf scraping across concrete. "My order has a saying too, and it's roughly translated as, 'The gods provide'. Do you understand what that means, human?"

Alistair nodded.

"I thought so. It isn't so complicated that other species couldn't grasp it if they only listened. The gods provide, and they've done so yet again."

Alistair felt the hair on Ob's neck rise.

"No doubt, you've seen those three dark creatures coming for you. The things that are all tentacle and filled with hunger?"

Alistair closed his eyes and remembered what he'd seen on the holovid. The black beasts that had destroyed his ships, killing so many inside. With his eyes closed, he said, "I know of them."

"Well, they're here. They've finally found you, though without our assistance, they can't come any closer to our world. They wait outside an invisible line of demarcation that allows them to avoid harm. It's clear they don't understand what's to come when the star collapses in on itself; otherwise, they'd wait much farther away. However, the gods have provided us a way to understand their will."

Alistair didn't need to hear the rest to know what the creature meant, yet the alien continued. "We will send you out to meet your hunters, you and your animal. If you survive, then the gods meant this place to be only a brief stop on your journey. If you don't survive, well, then the gods' will has triumphed. Do you understand, human?"

He wanted to scream at these creatures. He wanted to leap to wherever they sat and rip them apart with his bare hands. They were going to send him and Obs out in a tiny ship to fight the black creatures that ate metal as if it were butter? They might as well send the ship into their star.

"The ship will shield you from the radiation," the older voice said. "It's imperative that you leave immediately, though, because if you win against these creatures, you will still need to get past the pull of the black hole. Like I said, they aren't far away enough to avoid that. Do you accept our terms of discovering the gods' will?"

"My Whip. I need it. Not for the battle with these things, but for the next one."

He heard another chuckle snake around the room, though this one more good-natured than the others. "We are not thieves, human. The Whip has been with you this entire time."

Alistair felt it. The weapon sat on his hip and most likely had been there since he'd put on the clothes they gave him. He just hadn't been able to feel it.

He couldn't stop his hand from grabbing it, and the Whip immediately unfurled, working as it had the day he'd received it. The red lasers lit up much of the room, and Alistair stared around as it dangled by his feet. He could barely make out the creatures above him.

He only needed a moment to know they were right; he didn't want to view them.

Obs whimpered as Alistair turned off the Whip and

hooked it to his waistline again. He closed his eyes, trying to force away the vision of the creatures, but knew he'd never be able to forget. To see them fully? Surely he would have gone mad.

The drathe leaned harder against him.

The next laugh brought goosebumps to Alistair's spine. "You and all those like you are a stubborn breed. We tried to shield you from something you couldn't handle, but you refused to accept our orders, even those issued for your good. I think the gods brought you here to die, and I think we'll see that soon enough. Go now, Alistair Kane, and find out if the gods will provide for you."

Alistair had been led back to his room, though with his Whip, he probably could have made it on his own. The first alien walked in front of him as if nothing had changed despite the red light shining both forward and backward down the hallway.

The stranger could probably dim the Whip's light if he wanted, but he acted as if he couldn't sense it.

They reached Alistair's room. His MechSuit was waiting for him, sitting on the floor in front of his cot. "When do I leave?" he asked as he stepped in.

"As soon as you put that on," the stranger remarked. "Our calculations of the black hole are breaking down. It's mostly a guess now. It honestly could happen any second. Who can tell these things besides the gods? Put that on, then I am to take you to your ship."

Alistair placed the Whip on the cot, then stepped into the suit's boots. It immediately began unfolding around him, metal sliding on metal as it rose to the full height of his body. When it finished, he picked up his Whip and slapped it on the belt. "How about your calculations on that ship? Is it going to protect us from the radiation?"

The alien monk looked much smaller now that Alistair wore the MechSuit. He checked the place where Gracilis had stabbed him, finding it healed just as his shoulder had been.

"We think it will protect you, but again, you are in the hands of the gods now, not us."

Alistair didn't care to hear any more from these creatures. They'd given him his only chance of survival, and despite it being slim, he was ready to take it. "Let's go. Take us to the ship."

They went through the halls silently. Alistair felt true anger at this strange, disgusting species. They had acted pious, all the while playing gods. He could not fathom the audacity it took to think you could understand the gods, and in doing so, they'd nearly killed him. Perhaps they had killed him, depending on what came next.

They reached the ship. It could comfortably house the two of them, but for how long? Alistair didn't know. "What are the provisions like on this? Water and food? What kind of fuel does it use?"

The stranger replied softly, "You have enough water and food to last a standard Earth year. Don't worry about the fuel. The ship will continue to move as long as you tell it to."

Alistair was dismissive at this point. "Does it come with any kind of artificial intelligence?"

The alien nodded. "There's an AI on board to assist."

Alistair knew he was no pilot. He'd almost died a little while back when he'd tried to be, so the AI was a necessity if he was going to get out of this. He doubted it would be of much use to him in the battle with the AllSeer's creatures, though.

Alistair opened the ship's side door and Obs stepped in, immediately beginning to sniff the structures. The drathe hadn't shown any fear after they'd left the aliens the Whip had revealed, though he'd done his best to stay away from the stranger leading them. He understood what they truly were, and he wanted nothing to do with them.

The animal knew what was coming as well, and he hadn't shown any fear of that either. He was ready to get off this doomed planet.

Alistair watched him explore the ship for a few moments, awed by the beast's faith in him. He didn't care that the two of them were going to face creatures that crushed ships. He and his master would be fine. The belief radiated off him.

"If you'll permit, Kane, I'd like to say something before you leave."

Alistair's helmet was tucked into the neckline, and he raised his eyebrows in surprise as he turned to look at the alien. "You all haven't said enough? What is it?"

"The elder, the one who made the final decision, he believes the gods intend you to die here with us. There were very few who believed differently. I was one of them, and it was my idea to see what would happen with these entities waiting for you." The stranger didn't hide his blind face but stared ahead as if he saw everything with the holes. "Maybe the gods didn't mean for you to die here as you said. I don't know. I do have some advice about these things you're going to face. Would you permit me to give it?"

"Hurry," Alistair said. "Time isn't getting longer for us."

"Whatever you think of my kind, acceptance is truly the separation between you and me. I accept what is given to me, and you refuse to. I am going to my death without fear because I know I don't understand everything. The weapon you carry on your hip and the ship you're stepping into, neither of those is going to save you from the tentacled things. Perhaps, though, if you stop fighting and just accept the world as it is, the gods will spare you."

Alistair stared at the blind monk with a mixture of hatred and pity. "Walk with your kind into oblivion, monk. I've got things to do."

The stranger nodded, showing no emotion, and strode away from the landing bay, extinguishing the lamp as he did. Alistair pulled his Whip from his belt and lit the area around him. "All right, Obs. Not much time left, so we've got to hurry." He shortened the three strands of his Whip as he stepped into the ship, locating the cockpit quickly.

The lights flashed on, and the ship purred to life within a few minutes.

"Obs, you know the drill," Alistair told him.

The drathe sauntered over to the seat next to his master's and hopped onto it. Alistair took a minute to strap the animal in, then once again turned his attention to the ship's bow.

The landing bay door was closed and they were deep inside the planet, which kept the harmful radiation from destroying their cells.

That was only for the moment, though.

"Alistair Kane?" It was the AI's voice coming through the intercom system.

"That's me. You go by anything?"

"It's been a very long time since I've been used," the AI responded. "You can call me whatever you like."

"AI fits just fine for me," Alistair responded. "What are your programmed orders?" He figured the aliens would not allow him to try to avoid the AllSeer's kill-beasts, though it wasn't like he'd be able to get far in this ship anyway.

"I am to take you directly and without any deviation to the three beings waiting at the radiation demarcation line. If we survive that encounter, I'm programmed to get you away from the coming gravity crunch. If we survive that, I'm programmed to do whatever you want."

"'Lot of ifs in that programming," Alistair said. "Let's get moving, AI. Daylight is burning, after all."

The AI chuckled. "I understand that reference. I am a human-created intelligence. The species here would not have understood."

Alistair looked at Obs with wide eyes. "Look, AI, if we survive all this like you said, we can discuss anything you want. Right now, get me to those tentacled freaks, got it?"

"Certainly."

The door in front of them opened, and the ship rushed forward.

Alistair gripped the armrests as the speed increased.

Obs' body was pushed back against the seat. "AI, are we going to make it out of this planet?" Alistair yelled as they got closer to the bay door.

"Certainly," it answered.

The ship breached the door and immediately swung upward. Had it proceeded forward another inch, it would have been crushed against a steel wall. Alistair stared out, watching as the ship flew through the tunnel leading to the planet's poisonous atmosphere.

The steel next to Alistair whipped by in a blur. The brilliant hues of the star and gray surrounded him.

Moments later, they reached the planet's surface.

The star's radiance dimmed as the aliens' technology took over, and the interior of the ship darkened. Alistair looked at Obs to see how the animal was doing. His eyes were closed, but Alistair saw nothing burning on him. The radiation wasn't getting through, at least not yet.

"AI, how long until we make contact?"

"I'll have us there in two standard hours."

"What's our weapons loadout like on this thing? What kind of firepower are we working with?"

"The ship is equipped with lasers, plasma, and turrets. I'm capable of handling them all at the same time."

"That's better than nothing," Alistair responded. "What I want you to do is remain just far enough behind the radiation line that the creatures can't get to us without harming themselves. We'll try to shoot 'em down from there."

"I've been studying these creatures since I received my programming," the AI said. "Their speed and agility are unlike anything I've ever encountered. If I can't hurt them from that distance, what would you like me to do next?"

Alistair leaned back in his chair and retracted the armor on his hands. He rested his right on Ob's hindquarters and closed his eyes.

He was glad to be away from the moronic aliens masquerading as monks, but he understood he was heading toward his death. All the weapons on this ship would mean little when they got to these creatures.

The Prometheus Hunters.

The tentacled things sensed that they were near their prey. They'd sniffed him out from across the universe, and when they'd finally reached the planet he resided on, they could barely contain their excitement. When first sensing he was this close, they rushed directly toward the planet and the dying star. Their tentacles had burned off before they understood they couldn't get to their quarry.

They'd turned back to where the radiation couldn't harm their bodies and allowed themselves to heal.

Something was different about this place; they were certain of that, though they didn't have the intelligence to determine what it was. They only knew that to go forward would kill them, and that was a condition they'd never before encountered.

They waited, and when they sensed their prey moving, their newly born limbs started twitching with anticipation.

Perhaps the one they chased might try to escape,

though that worried them little. They'd found him here; they could find him anywhere.

Having traveled untold light-years, the three creatures watched as the ship carrying their prey turned *toward* them.

They were ecstatic. This was what they'd been created for: to kill the man who was coming to meet them.

CHAPTER THIRTEEN

As Alistair headed toward three creatures that wanted to kill him, Thoreaux donned his war gear.

The gigantes and the fleet of ships carrying them hung above Neptune. They hadn't dropped out of the fifth dimension yet, but the Neptunians knew they were there. The gigantes could remain there as long as Thoreaux wanted them to, but at some point, this battle had to begin.

The strategy was set, the troops ready.

Thoreaux put on the armor the Terram had provided for him—the FireStarter. He hooked the gauntlets on his arms, watching as they melded with the armor on his shoulders. He knew the Neptunians were small in stature, but he also understood it wouldn't just be Neptunians fighting. There would be Earthborn and people from other planets as well.

The Neptunians might be small, but they were hard people. Thoreaux would forget that at his peril.

Faitrin sat across the room, watching as he dressed.

Thoreaux could have started the battle yesterday, but

he'd decided to hold off one more day. He didn't lie about the reason why: he was waiting for Prometheus. Hoping against all hope, he'd thought that perhaps Pro would show up.

He hadn't.

"You can wait another day, ya know?" Faitrin said. She wasn't dressed for war yet, though Thoreaux knew she'd start soon. "There's no rule that says we can't wait one more day."

He nodded as he clicked the gauntlet on his left arm together. "I know, but there's a horde of gigantes sitting in an upper dimension, waiting for my signal. Prometheus isn't coming back here. Waiting won't help us. It'll only give the Commonwealth more time to prepare."

Faitrin was quiet for a moment, then said, "You've got to go across first? There's no way you can wait for a later group, even the AllMother's?"

Thoreaux said nothing as he moved to the table that held his beam. He placed the pistol on the suit's belt, then took two sabers and hooked them as well. He rarely fought with sabers; he preferred using ranged weapons, but there wasn't any telling what he'd need once he crossed through the portal.

"Did you hear me?" Faitrin asked.

"I heard you, love," he whispered without looking at her. "I wish I could go later, but right now, I've got to take his spot. He'd be on the front lines, and that's what everyone needs to witness. That's where I've got to be."

"I can't be there with you? There's no way?"

A small grin appeared on Thoreaux's face. "I probably don't tell you enough that I love you." He turned to look at her. "The last time you fought hand-to-hand, one of the gigantes nearly killed you. Did you forget that?"

She shrugged, grinning back. "I was hoping everyone else had. You weren't even there, so you can't know for certain. That could all just be rumors."

They weren't rumors, and both of them knew it. When Prometheus had gone to save Thoreaux, Faitrin had nearly been killed. It was only Caesar's nanotech that had saved her when he switched allegiance after seeing Pro fight.

"I can't be worried about you while I'm fighting the Commonwealth. Plus, I need you up above keeping me alive. You know that."

Faitrin stood and crossed the short distance between them. "I do. I'm just scared."

Thoreaux leaned his forehead against his lover's. "I am too. I think I'd be scared even if Pro was here."

Faitrin raised her hands and cupped Thoreaux's face, their heads still touching. "We're going to be okay. I might be scared, but I do believe that. He picked us for a reason. He and the AllMother knew what they were doing."

"I'm hoping so," Thoreaux said. "We're crossing in three hours. You need to suit up."

Faitrin smiled. "Sir, yes, sir."

For the first time, Alistair saw them with his own eyes. They were still far in the distance, but the ship's AI had highlighted them. They were zipping back and forth across the sky, always seeming to look at him.

It reminded Alistair of the way Thoreaux paced.

"Enlarge the view," he told the AI.

The screen in front of him zoomed in, giving him a much better view of the creatures he'd be facing soon. Each one was at least as big as the ship he was traveling in, their tentacles easily able to stretch from one end to the other.

"Bring the ship to a stop," he told the AI.

"Are you sure? We're nearly in range to begin our attack," the AI responded.

"I'm sure." Alistair had to stop the ship, but he didn't know why. Sometimes he hated the powers the AllMother had given him, and this was one of those times. He felt something was about to happen, but he didn't know what. His mind could tell that not everything was as it should be, but it couldn't detect the difference.

Obs turned in his chair and whined, not liking how his master was behaving.

Alistair stared at the squid-like creatures, though he wasn't seeing them. "It's okay, boy."

I've felt this before, he thought, *but it isn't possible. Not anymore.*

What was impossible out here in space with these creatures and a collapsing star?

He knew what was different, and he knew what was coming to him: the AllMother.

Somehow, against all odds, she was racing toward him, or her mind was.

"AI, I don't know how hard this is going to hit me. You keep this ship here until I tell you otherwise." Alistair had been knocked on his ass many times by the AllMother's strength, and if she was somehow sending him a message out here, he didn't know if he'd remain conscious once he received it.

Closer now, he thought. *Almost here.*

He gritted his teeth, grabbed the armrests of his chair, and stared blindly into space. He was prepared for the AllMother.

It hit him like the smallest breath of air, as if a newborn baby were resting on his shoulder and breathing through its nose. If Alistair hadn't prepared, he might have missed it; that was how weak her presence was.

Prometheus, get to Neptune. We need you.

The last word was barely intelligible, yet Alistair heard it. He didn't understand how she'd found him or if he had stumbled across the message. Regardless of how it had reached him, it was the AllMother.

He was needed on Neptune, and that could only mean one thing: Thoreaux was going ahead with the war. It took only a few seconds for Alistair to outline the plan Thoreaux would be using. He'd sent the gigantes and some of the Monaham hybrids to the Solar System through the fifth dimension. Meanwhile, he and the ground troops would cross through the portal on Phoenix and attempt to take Neptune, which was the planet farthest from Earth.

Alistair nodded. *Not bad, Thoreaux. Not too bad.*

It wasn't grand either because the AllMother had wasted all she had left to send him that message. Did they know where he was but couldn't get here, or had the AllMother thrown little more than a prayer to the gods?

The AI spoke from the intercom. "Are you okay, Alistair Kane?"

He nodded as his grip on the armrests weakened. "I'm fine."

"Do you want me to continue waiting here?" The AI paused. "The fluctuations from the star are outside predicted variations. We should decide our plan of action and commit soon."

Alistair didn't need to be a physicist or astronomer to know what the AI meant. It was the same thing the alien had told him. At this moment, the predicted behavior of the star was just the best guess. They couldn't say for sure what it would do, and the fluctuations most likely weren't a good thing, not for anyone who wanted to continue living.

The star was about to collapse.

Thoreaux was about to go to war.

Alistair was looking at three creatures who'd crossed galaxies to kill him and meant to do it right now.

Obs whined again, either sensing his master's unease or a change in gravity.

Alistair continued staring out. "What do you think these fluctuations mean? Best estimate is fine," he told the AI.

"It's running out of fuel and is going to attempt to expand within the next hour. It won't have the mass, and it's going to collapse. Everything around it will collapse as well."

Alistair nodded. They had one hour. The aliens had been off by a good bit. Hopefully, they understood their gods as well as they understood this star. "If we didn't have these creatures in front of us, would we be able to escape the collapse within an hour?"

"No. We are too close. We will either die as it expands or fall into the black hole created when it fails."

Alistair nodded again. Obs was staring intently at his master.

Alistair thought back to what the alien had said to him. The gist of it had been that humans refuse to accept their fate. They were always striving for something greater or wishing to get rid of something they hated.

They couldn't simply accept reality for what it was.

Alistair didn't know if that was humanity's greatest strength or weakness, but he understood that right now, there wasn't a choice but for him to accept.

Was it the will of the gods he was accepting, or was it reality? Was there a difference? He'd been brought up to believe the gods were long gone if they'd ever existed.

What had the AllMother told him when he was preparing for the Ice Queen? A great wind was carrying him, even when he didn't know it. Was that similar to what the alien had told him? In some ways, yes.

Alistair listed the facts very simply. The creatures in front of him would chase him until the end of time or until their deaths. He could not escape the star's destruction. He didn't know how he'd gotten to this star system. Thoreaux and the rest of his family needed him.

A great wind had carried him before and was perhaps still carrying him.

Or maybe his time in the universe had ended.

Either way, he needed to accept that he wasn't leaving this star system without the great wind. He didn't have to accept that these murderous creatures would remain in the universe.

The AI broke the lengthy silence. "Sir?"

"You're programmed to listen to my directions as long as I don't try to escape the creatures in front of me, correct?"

"That is correct," it answered him.

"Okay, then listen very carefully," Alistair said with a small, sly grin on his face.

Obs whined again.

The hour was upon them.

Thoreaux had just finished his last communication with the gigantes floating in the fifth dimension near Neptune. They were ready and would attack at the right time.

Pro's council knew their places and positions. They would unfurl at the right times like Pro's Whip did.

The cavern that held Phoenix's portal was full of soldiers, men and women ready to die if need be. A few short weeks ago, Thoreaux had seen his leader tossed through the portal, unable to save him.

Now Thoreaux stood above the packed cavern. This would be the first wave, the one Thoreaux would lead onto the foreign planet.

He stepped up to the rock rail and looked at his soldiers. A shiver ran down his spine. He'd watched Prometheus do this, but he'd never had the opportunity to do it himself. He'd never wanted to.

He didn't have his helmet on, though the rest of his armor was in place. The comm at the top of his neck plate would send his voice to the multitudes beneath.

"All of you know who I am," he said, hearing his voice echo off the rock walls around him. "You all know I'm not the one who is supposed to be standing here. I cannot tell you where Prometheus is. I just know he's not here, and I know what my duty is: to continue his quest to overthrow the Commonwealth."

Thoreaux looked at his armored feet for a second. The cavern was eerily silent, given all the people standing in it.

"I have faith in Prometheus; I know he's coming. I've seen him rise and rise again, regardless of the forces before him, and this time will be no different." He looked up, anger rising in his chest. His lip peeled back in a snarl. "It's my job—it's *our* job—to be there when he arrives, so if any of you wonder if we can win, do *not* go through that portal. Stay here and wait until our victory has been secured. I won't lead people who doubt. I'm not our savior. I'm only preparing the way for him when he arrives."

He unhooked the armor on his left forearm. It collapsed into a bracelet, and Thoreaux snapped it onto his belt before grabbing the blade next to it.

"Prometheus taught me this. He taught us all this. This is how we go to war since we should not fear anything."

He held his arm above the railing so all could see it.

"I do not kill for glory!" he shouted to the masses.

Their voice came back as one, repeating his words. Repeating Prometheus' words.

"I do not kill for malice! I kill because it is right! Because if I do not kill, those who seek to harm me and those I love will do so!"

Thoreaux grabbed the blade, just as he'd seen

153

Prometheus do so many times. He brought the business end to his flesh and dragged it across. Blood sprang out and dripped on the people beneath.

Those it dropped on didn't look up. They were too busy cutting into their flesh.

"I do not fear the enemy!" Thoreaux yelled. "I do not fear death! I only fear living without protecting those I love! I only fear cowardice and hiding from my duty! As this blood flows, so will I. I bleed now so that I will not bleed later. I bleed now so that those who sow harm against me know that blood does not frighten me. I bleed now because it is this blood that will conquer anyone in my path. See it and fear! See it and die!"

The roar from beneath Thoreaux rose until his eardrums rang.

Prometheus would come.

Until then, the Commonwealth's blood would flow, and when he arrived, streets full of red liquid would greet him.

CHAPTER FOURTEEN

"What I'd give to be a machine right now," Ares grumbled.
"I'd even consider giving up my dick and the chance to
ever have sex again to not feel this damned fourth
dimension."

They hadn't dropped out of the fourth dimension since
they'd taken off, and Ares' unmodified body was feeling the
effects.

He and Monk had remained in the never-ending
prison, the doors always opening to another room. No
other prisoners had joined them, and Ares was beginning
to see how the sheer monotony of this life could drive
someone insane.

Ares hadn't seen Veena since they left, and only Monk
was able to tell how many days had passed since they'd
boarded this ship. Ares had stopped asking, though. Right
now, his body *hurt*, and he had no idea how long it would
be forced to continue like this.

If the AllSeer hadn't needed what was in his mind, his

and Veena's, they surely would have been in the fifth dimension long ago.

At the moment, Monk was on the other side of the room, positioned as if he were staring at the wall. Ares knew him well enough to understand the machine was hacking something. He did this from time to time, and when he finished, Ares would ask what he'd found out.

The normal answer was along the lines of, "We're on a need-to-know basis, human, and right now, you don't need to know anything."

Ares lay on his side and was staring at Monk's back when something new and shocking happened.

Monk's head turned one-hundred-and-eighty degrees so he was looking at Ares, but his body still faced the wall. Monk had never done that before, though the ability had probably always been there. He most likely didn't do it because it unnerved humans, who were incapable of such movement.

The blue light atop his head turned on, signaling that he was stealthing the area. Monk rarely did that anymore since he thought the ship was too advanced to continually use the technology.

"Something is happening," Monk said without any of the sarcasm or annoyance that usually infused his voice.

Ares swung his legs off the bed and sat up, forgetting the pain that pressed on his body. "Where? What? Is Veena okay?"

"It's Kane," the robot said. "I'm with the AllSeer's creatures right now, and they're staring at him." His voice sounded as if he were reading off a holoprompter, the words flowing through him without thought. "He's in a ship in front of a star in the last stages of its life. They want him, the creatures. They're willing to do almost anything to get him, but they understand that venturing past a certain place will leave them vulnerable to radiation."

Ares had stood without realizing it. "Is Alistair okay?"

The machine paused. "He's about to do something very stupid. The only comparable human action is suicide. He is about to commit suicide."

Ares took a deep breath and let it out slowly, then sat back on the bed. He carefully laid back down on his side, the pain in his body creeping back into his consciousness. "No, that's just Alistair about to win. Let me know when he does. For now, I'm going to focus on how bad I hurt and how much I hate you and everything else."

The AllSeer was alone in a room that was quite different from the rest of his dreadnought. It bore the same colors as the armor covering his body, black and green, though the green moved gently across the walls, floors, and ceiling in waves.

The room wasn't large, perhaps ten meters by ten meters. No one else came into it besides the AllSeer, and only when he needed to be somewhere else. It was how he had been able to meet the Prophesied One, to see him almost face to face. This room and a similar one on his homeworld allowed him to travel across galaxies without taking a step.

The AllSeer knew his creations had finally found the Prophesied One.

He'd somehow been separated from the AllSeer's sister and the rest of her people. The AllSeer didn't know how it had happened, and at the moment, he wasn't concerned about it.

The AllSeer was lying on his back facing the ceiling, but the floor had melded with him like mushrooms do as they latch onto deadwood. It was hard to tell where the room ended and the AllSeer began. It had attached to his back, buttocks, and legs, as well as the backs of his arms. That hadn't been enough for the room, though, and it had also started to grow up and around the mutant's body as if it wanted to consume him.

Only the AllSeer's body was in the ship. His mind, his *being*, was with his creations.

He'd transported to where they awaited the Prophesied One. The AllSeer saw the ship, just as a certain machine did in another part of the ship.

Where the machine saw insanity, the AllSeer saw something different.

The difference between us, Prophesied One, is bloodline, he thought as he stared at Alistair Kane's insane gambit for life. *Only your bloodline will keep you from succeeding here where I would have. You were a worthy opponent.*

He didn't need to see anything else, already understanding how Kane's maneuver would play out. The floor began retracting from him, and his mind returned to the ship.

With the Prophesied One gone, there was nothing separating him from his sister.

They would reunite on Neptune, then make their way to Earth, a homecoming for all to see.

CHAPTER FIFTEEN

Dominik had donned the armor of his ancestors, those who had come to Neptune hundreds of years ago to conquer a planet that was made predominately of gas. They'd called it a gas giant back then. Now it was only a giant.

He wasn't wearing the MechSuit of the Titans or the Martian armor that he'd recently seen on the mutant Hector de Gracilis. No, his armor was Neptunian, and even with the technological upgrades that had occurred over the years, the gray metal, which was covered with small circular lights at the joints, was distinctively Neptunian.

The gray symbolized the brutal wind of the planet, and the lights had been used by the first men to explore the gas giant. They could see nothing this far out, so lights were in case someone found themselves lost.

Lights were needed to recover the bodies of those who died terraforming the planet.

The current form of them could be extinguished with a single word inside the helmet in case they became a liability during battle. Dominik liked to see them, though, and he was anxious to view them on the field of battle in the next few hours.

He wanted these Subversives to see them and realize the mistake they'd made.

His people continually scanned the fifth dimension; Dominik had known within thirty minutes that the fleet was in attack range. Since then, every half-hour, he'd received updates on their movement. Their strategy wasn't hard to discern, at least the overarching one. The Subversives would maintain a primary group above the portal to support those who came through. Dominik also thought they'd have two tertiary forces that would attempt to put pressure on the Neptunians to protect their populated areas. The tertiary forces would rely on speed to move faster than the ground forces.

Neptune didn't lack ships, though, and Dominik had a plan in place to chase each one of those tertiary aircraft down and destroy them. The Subversives were low people, perhaps the lowest form of human to ever exist. He wasn't surprised they would attack civilians, though he was disgusted by it.

As of now, the Subversive fleet wasn't moving. It remained relatively stationary in the fifth dimension, but Dominik knew the moment they started dropping dimensions, the war was upon them.

He found his thoughts going to the Martian the Imperial Ascendant had sent to die. Dominik understood why the Ascendant would shove him onto the frontlines. He'd seen Hector de Gracilis on Earth when de Finita had called all the propraetors to humanity's first home. It was clear that Caius was playing the Imperial Ascendant, hoping to ride the mutant's coattails from Mars to Earth and never leave.

Dominik had heard about what the man did on Phoenix. He'd been like a force of nature, ripping through the planet with a Titan at his side; a Titan anyone could see had been put there to relay information to de Finita. Yet, the force of nature had met another force at the very end, and the mutant hadn't fared as well as everyone had thought he would against the mighty Prometheus.

Dominik had seen Hector a few hours ago, and although his face had been fixed, the rumor was Kane had damaged it badly. The rumor said Hector would have died if not for the Ascendant's Titan.

As Neptune's propraetor, Dominik had no interest in political games. He'd known Caius for a long time, and the man had risen high for someone who'd come from so low. His ambition would surely get him and his grandson killed.

Do I need him to live? Dominik wondered. He leaned forward in his chair, placing his elbows on his knees. *The Ascendant might want him dead, but does the Ascendant care if Neptune survives?*

The answer to that was no, under certain specific circumstances. De Finita was supremely arrogant, and he hadn't earned it. Perhaps his forebears had, but not him. He would sacrifice Neptune and all the people on it to eliminate the internal threat to his reign, the de Gracilis family. Dominik figured the Ascendant couldn't comprehend losing to this group of rebels.

The real question facing the propraetor was whether he needed Hector to ensure his people didn't die. Neptune had to stand. Dominik would not be the first of his lineage to lose what had been won with blood and steel.

On Earth, the Ascendant could proclaim what he wished. Here on Neptune, Dominik's word was final.

Hector's transport was racing over Neptune's surface, heading for the portal. The defending armies had been encamped for days, waiting for the battle to start, though everything was at a standstill right now.

Petra sat next to Hector, the Titan rarely leaving his side since he'd emerged from surgery.

He'd decided this morning that it was time to get to the front lines. Most of the Martian soldiers were already there, but Hector and Petra had traveled back and forth between the portal and Neptune's capital Trilonia over the past few days.

The transport was fast enough to get them to the battle within an hour as long as they remained in Trilonia. Hector felt the war was about to begin, though he couldn't tell Petra why when she'd asked. It was just something he felt in his bones. The shrieks of battle were near.

The transport operated on autopilot, and he looked out at the barren world. He could see mountains in the distance and knew that beyond them was one of the planet's three major oceans. This was his first time on Neptune, though he'd studied the planet as a boy. He'd known about the portal out here in the desert, though Neptunians hadn't. Many of the Commonwealth's lies were coming to the surface; regardless of what else Kane accomplished, he was certainly doing that.

The Commonwealth's reign was changing in his wake, Hector thought.

Petra had her MechSuit on, everything but the helmet, which remained rolled into the neck. "Are you thinking about him?" she asked.

Hector's eyes didn't leave the mountain ridges. He found it odd that she was coming to know him so well. Or, if not odd, disarming. "Are you?"

"Do you think he's dead?"

Hector felt her eyes on him, so he shook his head.

"Do you think he's going to show up here? Is this some kind of trick?"

Hector scratched the side of his face. He hadn't shaved in two days, and his usually smooth face was grizzled. "I think he's coming, yes, but I don't think it's a trick."

"Why not?" Petra asked.

She was one of the few people who could ask Hector questions like that. He knew most people found him unapproachable, not only because of his size but also his demeanor. Most people didn't ask, and if they did, Hector ignored them. Besides his grandfather, of course. He kept his thoughts to himself. Yet with Petra, he didn't mind the question, and he shared openly even though he knew she was most likely reporting to the Ascendant.

"I think this thing, this insurrection, is spiraling out of control. Out of our control, out of his, out of the Ascendant's. I tossed him through that portal on Phoenix, but he didn't go where he should have. I've studied the data. No one in this galaxy has any idea where he went, and I don't think anyone in his rebellion does either."

Petra paused, and when she did speak, her question came out slowly. "What are you saying?"

"No one's in control of this war, and anyone who thinks they are is only fooling themselves. There are powers in play I can't fathom, and I don't think Kane can either. He isn't dead, but I think the powers I can't fathom are on his side. I think he'll show up here; I'm just not sure how or when."

Hector hadn't even given his grandfather that information. He wondered if the Ascendant was listening to him now and what the ruler would think if he was.

The transport's AI spoke through the dashboard. "Dominik de Febian would like to speak to you privately, Hector de Gracilis."

It was a simple AI that facilitated travel from point A to point B as well as transmitting messages.

Hector looked at Petra, but her helmet was rolling up around her head. She planned on turning the sound off inside so she couldn't hear what the two men said.

Hector shook his head. "You can listen. I'm sure you know I don't fear de Finita. What you tell him is up to you. I'd rather the person next to me know what I know so when hard decisions need to be made, we move as one."

The helmet quit rolling up, pausing and framing Petra's shock at Hector's words. It was the first time he'd mentioned the relationship between her and de Finita.

After a moment, the Titan regained control of her face and rolled the helmet back into the suit's neckline.

"Put him through," Hector told the AI.

A holovid jumped up between Hector and Petra. It was the propraetor, who was seated and had most of his Neptunian armor on. The lights at his shoulder joints shone brightly, circling beneath his armpit and above his shoulder.

Hector spoke first. "Forgive me, Propraetor, but anything you wish to say to me, I must request you allow Petra to hear it as well. She has saved my life before, and I cannot leave her in the dark as we head to battle."

Dominik looked at Petra for a moment, the holovid on his side displaying the two of them as they sped over barren rock. He turned back to Hector. "As you wish. I'm sure you understand the risk. We've discussed your orders from the Ascendant. You're to remain on the front line. I've been giving this some thought, and while I see the wisdom of the Ascendant's orders, there might be things on the battlefield we should change. I'm coming shortly, but I want you to obey me as propraetor of this planet, direct envoy of the Imperial Ascendant, and commander of this army. If I say you need to leave the front line, I expect you to listen to me. Is that understood?"

Hector turned his gaze to the passing landscape again. "I understand, Propraetor."

"Good. One People. One Purpose."

"One People. One Purpose," Hector and Petra chanted in unison.

The holovid went dead, and they were alone again.

"You understand the game that's afoot?" Hector asked without looking over.

"The Ascendant plans on you dying at the portal. He isn't planning on my death, or rather, it'll be incidental.

The propraetor thinks you might be needed if the war doesn't end at the portal. If so, he doesn't plan on letting you die."

Hector nodded. "That's the gist of it, yes." He turned to Petra and looked her in the eye. "Warriors are nothing but pieces to be moved in a game. Those playing the game will kill or save us, depending on what they need. De Febian is no different than de Finita, and neither is different than de Gracilis. Now we are pieces, but one day, if we survive their games, we will move them."

Petra shook her head. "I don't want to move men as pieces."

Hector smiled at the woman. She was just barely not a girl, at least in age. "That is why you'd be a great person to do so." He turned back to the window. "Enough talk. Prepare for war. It'll be here soon."

CHAPTER SIXTEEN

Thoreaux stood in line with thousands of others. Relm was on his right, and Nero was on Relm's right. Both wore their helmets, but Relm had traded his MechPulse for Monaham gloves. Thoreaux had learned their name, but at that moment, pressed together and staring at a portal, he couldn't remember what they were called.

Sweat dripped down his face inside his helmet. The heat of the planet's core, combined with the sheer number of bodies and the knowledge of what was to come, would make anyone sweat.

"You know your role, right?" Thoreaux asked Relm through a private comm.

"I got it, broth. I'm to get the giant, then the two giants, and I will come to save everyone. Just make sure there's something left to be saved, 'kay?"

Thoreaux nodded in answer.

He switched his comm to the first wave, ready to communicate to thousands.

"On my command.

"Three."

"Two."

"Go."

Thoreaux rushed forward, the soldiers to his right and left running as fast as he. He didn't think of Faitrin or Prometheus when he reached the arch. He remembered Hel. He remembered what the Commonwealth had done to him.

He broke the portal's plane and felt the familiar disorientation of moving through a controlled black hole. There was a brief but intense moment of pain as if his body was compressed to a single point, then he was past it, and his foot hit solid ground.

Thoreaux was on Neptune.

The disorientation faded quickly, and the dim light of the sun showed the armies in front of him.

Forward! his mind shouted, knowing troops were directly behind him.

He started running, raising his MechPulse and blasting. Lasers rushed past him, some too high, some too low, and some taking his compatriots' heads off.

Thoreaux looked to his right, where Relm and Nero were firing.

Good, he thought, then the bloodlust overcame him.

Relm hadn't fought next to Nero before, and despite the gigante's size, he hadn't expected much. Nero was too goofy, too aloof, and too damned weird to be of much help in battle. That was what Relm originally thought, at least.

The two of them crashed through the portal at about the same time. Relm *never* adjusted to coming through as fast as other people, and he'd told Nero that before they entered the cavern.

"If you don't help me, I'm probably gonna end up blasted, broth. It takes me entirely too long to get my space legs under me, if you understand."

Nero had laughed and clapped him on the back with a huge, meaty hand. "No worry, Nero will take care of you."

Relm touched down on Neptune, and his hands went to his knees. He was going to puke, and there wasn't anything he could do about it. He tried to look at the enemy, but his body wouldn't allow it.

I'm going to die, he thought as the faceplate on his helmet rolled back and his mouth opened to vomit.

He started puking just as someone grabbed him by the shoulder and *threw* him.

The vomit streaked behind him as his body rushed forward, the ground blurring beneath him. He was just about to hit when he saw Nero's massive hand reach out of nowhere and set him on his feet.

A laser slashed by Nero's head, only about a half-meter away. The gigante didn't turn. "Are you ready now?"

Relm's eyes were wide, but he was reoriented. Puke dripped down his shoulder, yet no more was erupting from his throat. Eyes still wide, he nodded as his faceplate rolled back into place.

Nero wasted no time, pulling two sabers from his belt and rushing forward.

Inside his helmet, Relm blinked, letting the heads-up display tell him what he couldn't see. Thousands of warriors were to his left. Nero had gauged his throw perfectly, giving Relm just enough space to come to his senses without being overrun.

Not quite, he thought. Nero was raining Hades down on those around them. The nanotech was spreading from his hands, healing the wounds he received, but he was creating space to allow Relm to get himself together.

Let's go, broth, he told himself.

The gloves were on his hands, though they fit too snugly over the armor. He retracted the armor, freeing his hands. The moment he'd seen the banshees using them, he'd known they were a thousand times better than his MechPulse.

The blue substance flew from them, striking soldiers who had no idea what he was using. They paused, not understanding what was happening. This was a new weapon, something the Commonwealth had never come across before.

"LET'S GO, LITTLE MAN!" Nero screamed as he impaled someone with his saber.

Relm followed when the gigante moved farther to the right. The plan was simple, even if the execution was impossible.

Relm fired with his hands, using the gloves as he'd practiced. It wasn't like the MechPulse yet, but the damage was quicker, and the reload was instantaneous.

Relm dropped two men, blue substance grabbing their armor and melting through it to the skin. They didn't know to pull it off as Prometheus had. They simply burned.

Nero was still moving to the right, creating space. Relm glanced at the sky. A massive fleet appeared to be unfolding in the sky, the ships appearing to be coming from two-dimensional space to the third, though it was in the opposite direction. Huge blasts of plasma fell from the sky, aiming toward the back of the opposing force, trying not to hit friendlies.

Relm ran, following the giant's path as he supported from the back. There'd be a skimmer waiting for them that would hopefully bring them to the main city.

Screams, blasts, and explosions filled his senses. The fog of war wasn't something that only plagued those in charge; it overtook those fighting worse than anyone could imagine. Relm only knew to follow the giant leading the way. He was a god amongst mortals, and Relm could do nothing but watch his back.

The nanotechnology from Nero's hands was circling Relm, ready to heal his injuries, though there were none yet.

It felt like hours, but it was only minutes before they broke through the right side. Relm hadn't seen the Neptunian fleet drop out of the fourth dimension, but they were firing at Thoreaux's fleet. Yet the ships from the insurrection were descending, carrying gigantes who would wreak havoc on soldiers wearing only armor.

Relm saw the small skimmer, and despite the death surrounding him, wondered, *How in Hades is this big bastard going to fit in?*

Nero seemed not to care. He kept killing. He kept moving forward.

The skimmer door opened and Nero threw a soldier

with his left hand, the man flying meters through the air. The giant pointed at the open door. "Get in, little man!"

Relm quit trying to fight and ran as fast as his legs could carry him. In all his days, he'd never seen a war like this, with thousands and thousands flooding against each other. He slid into the skimmer, hitting the opposite door before stopping.

Nero climbed in, and the door automatically shut.

"Fun times," Nero proclaimed as the ship took off, already programmed. Lasers barely missed the stern as it rushed toward the city where hopefully, Caesar awaited.

Nero looked at Relm, who hadn't thought to pull his helmet back. "Anyone ever tell you you're not great at fighting?"

He was smiling as if a virus had taken over his brain, rendering him insane.

They were moving so fast, the crowd of warriors was a blur to their left.

"Faceplate up," Relm whispered. His helmet followed his orders. He stared at the mad giant to his left. "Remind me when we're finished here to tell you why Pro named you what he did."

The gigante laughed loudly. "Remind me to teach you how to fight. I tell you, this isn't the time to worry. This is the time for fun."

CHAPTER SEVENTEEN

Acceptance was key; Alistair understood that now. It might not be what the little alien monk had meant, but Alistair had accepted his place in this universe and knew there wasn't any way out of it.

He had to hope a wind was waiting for him, or everything was over.

Obs was strapped in and staring straight ahead. Fear gripped the animal because nothing else could happen to someone capable of feeling afraid.

"There is a one hundred percent chance of death," the AI said over the intercom. "There is no way out of this."

Alistair had spent the last thirty minutes fucking with the creatures, firing weapons at them just out of the reach of radiation. They dodged them easily, but Alistair understood lust when he saw it, and these things weren't machines. They wanted him, and his firing only increased the desire.

Five minutes ago, Prometheus had stepped forward. Alistair took his seat in the back of their shared mind to watch the show, no longer needed. Nerves of hot plasma were needed now. No doubt. No fear. A killing machine. Prometheus took control, and two minutes after that, he gave the command that sealed everyone's fate.

"Get close enough to make them chase us, then head for the star."

"Repeat command," the AI said.

"Make them chase us, then head for the star," Prometheus repeated.

"You will kill everyone," the AI responded.

"Am I breaking your programming? If not, do it."

Now they were flying toward the collapsing star. The three tentacled creatures were rushing toward his ship, unable to withstand their bloodlust regardless of the radiation.

The technology surrounding Prometheus didn't matter. He felt the gravity. It was pulling him off the ship, and metal creaked around his ears.

"Obs, close your eyes," he commanded. "AI, one percent visibility."

If he was going to die, he wanted to witness the beauty as he did.

The drathe shut his eyes quickly. The brilliant blaze of light reached the ship.

"They're gaining, sir," the AI said.

"Keep us away from them until the collapse. Display them."

A holovid appeared to his left. The radiation was eating the creatures, though their tentacles were trying to regrow.

The ship went high, and immediately, the creatures switched direction. It dipped low and they followed, always gaining, their speed beyond anything this ship could hope to match.

The ship was shuddering, the sound of metal bending growing louder by the minute.

"Death is near, sir," the AI said, its voice calm. "Would you like me to continue?"

"Get me as close to the center of the collapse as possible."

At that moment, everything the alien species had planned for happened. There was no possibility of Prometheus finishing his sentence.

The planets, the dust, the ship, the creatures, Prometheus, and Obs were pulled into gravity that could stop time.

Only one thing could escape. Prometheus didn't know if it was possible, but he sent the thought with as much force as he could.

I'm coming, Mother.

He could only hope that was true.

CHAPTER EIGHTEEN

The AllMother stood in a cavern with thousands around her. Servia and Faitrin flanked her, and a tight guard of white-haired hybrids surrounded them.

Every minute or so, they moved forward. The portal loomed in front of them, a gate that led to victory or death.

The AllMother stepped forward, following the people in front of her. Servia leaned over, the sounds of clanking armor and shuffling feet making it nearly impossible to hear anything else.

"You okay?"

"Be prepared to kill, girl. I didn't make it this far by worrying about an old lady at my side," the AllMother snapped.

Servia straightened, and they continued forward.

Ten meters from the portal. She could feel the pull of the manipulated black hole. Fear was upon her, as it had been so many other times. Now, more than ever, she could do nothing to fight back. She had to trust. She had to believe what she'd told Prometheus. A strong wind was carrying them.

A strong wind. Trust it. A strong wind is carrying you, old—

There wasn't any warning. There wasn't any great force to it.

There was simply his voice, the man she'd searched her whole life for.

I'm coming, Mother.

It was weak, as if she'd sent it and not the beast she had created. Even so, there wasn't any mistaking that voice. He'd heard her, and he'd responded.

Tears came to her eyes. The AllMother couldn't help herself. She grabbed Servia's hand, her wiry strength startling the woman through her armor.

"Be ready," the AllMother said, eyes shining. "Prometheus is coming. Wage war now like you've never done, daughter. Time is short, and he'll need us as much as we need him."

They reached the portal and stepped through to a planet in flames.

Thirty minutes had elapsed since Relm boarded the skimmer. Warships were passing them, heading in the opposite direction. None bothered to look at the little skimmer. They probably couldn't take their eyes off the magnificent destruction in front of them. The portal's stealth technology had been removed, and the battle could be seen for hundreds if not thousands of kilometers. Only the planet's curvature would stop someone from seeing the cause of so much death.

Relm had turned about fifteen minutes ago, then told himself not to do it again.

It was a war unlike any he'd seen. There were no buildings to shield the soldiers, no streets to flee into. All that existed behind him was a massive portal and open land for as far as the eye could see.

There was nothing to protect his friends besides what they'd brought with them.

Plasma poured out of the sky like rain. Lasers came from almost every direction like sightless fire and fell from above like deadly daggers.

Relm hadn't been able to make out any of the people, of course. They were much too far away for that.

It wasn't necessary, though. His people were there, and he wasn't.

"Nero," he said from the skimmer's right side. "You said it isn't time to worry about Pro. What about Thoreaux and everyone back there? Is it time to worry about them?"

He looked at the giant; he was always amazed by the creature's facial expressions. Relm spent his time around people who'd mastered their emotions. Their faces didn't change regardless of what they were told or who'd said it. Nero had none of that restraint. Whatever he thought traveled immediately to his face, and if one couldn't infer what he was thinking, he would shortly tell you.

Nero was honest when so much of the universe was anything but that.

It took the gigante at least a minute, his expression confused despite the deadly task ahead of him. He wasn't focusing on that, though, but somehow reading tea leaves that only he could see.

Nero turned his huge head to Relm. "What do you mean by worry?"

Relm started to say something but found he couldn't figure out how to explain it to Nero.

The gigante spoke for him, his words stilted in his second language but impactful. "If you mean, should you obsess over whether or not they're going to live, the answer is no. Worrying provides no advantage. It does nothing for you. If you mean, should you devise a strategy to try and save your friends, again I'd say you should not worry. As a soldier, you have your orders, and it is not your place to change those orders. Do not worry about them. It won't help."

The giant turned his head back to the landscape in front of him.

Relm nodded with his lips turned down, impressed by the gigante's evaluation yet still wanting an answer. "Fair enough. Let me ask it this way then, Nero: is there a chance I'll be extremely sad because my friends die during this war?"

Finally, the giant nodded. "I cannot see certainties, little one. The only one I ever saw was when the spaceman and I went to meet the Ice Queen, but even then, I saw my death happen, and it didn't. Is there a chance that all you know will be destroyed in the war behind us? Yes, of course. If you would like to think about that chance, then dive into the sadness early. By all means, do it. My point is, none of that is going to help us free Caesar, and we are ten minutes from where our brother waits for us. Maybe it would be wise to think about *that* rather than trying to use me to figure out whatever your monkey mind wants to worry about."

Relm couldn't help but smile. The fucking creature was right.

"You're a prick, ya know that?" Relm said with a huge grin on his face.

"Any time you want to compare pricks, let me know," Nero said. His eyes sparkled with mirth. "I'd be happy to drop my pants, little one."

Relm could only shake his head, still grinning.

The city that had been so small an hour ago was now large in the ship's window. Relm had been on Neptune's moons but not on the planet. When the first humans to reach the planet started terraforming, they had to create more moons by using the layers of methane, ammonia, and water that peeled away as the planet's temperature increased. The moons had contained more mass than Earth, which spurred the planet's terraformation as well as allowing for life on the moons.

The moons had also helped the AllMother's force to grow because they had been able to hide on them. That was the closest Relm had ever been to Neptune.

The city before him was larger than anything he'd ever seen in his life. Even the capital city of the gigantes' home-world didn't compare. Relm understood why, though; it was much easier to build up than out in a world like this. Better to control a small area well than a large area poorly.

The skimmer was whipping along about a half-meter above the ground, moving up and down as it tried to main-tain that distance. The two of them were cruising at three hundred and thirty kilometers per hour, and a sudden stop would mean death.

"Five minutes to entrance," Nero said.

Relm shot up straight in his seat. "Wait, what? We're going in at this fucking speed?"

Nero smiled. "Thoreaux didn't tell you everything, I take it?"

Relm's face showed his terror. "Tell me what? You and I were to make the plan when we got here. He doesn't know a damned thing about this city, and neither do you. There's no way to make a plan from fucking *Phoenix*."

Nero nodded without losing his smile. "I made the plan, little one. We aren't slowing, and we're not stopping for anything. We will ride this skimmer until someone kills us or we arrive at the propraetor's residence."

"We won't make it," Relm interrupted. "A skimmer isn't built for city movement, especially not at this speed."

"Unfortunately, little one, you and I aren't made for this city movement either." He pointed. Before them were massive gates that stood taller than most buildings on the planet's moons. They were open, likely to allow the warships to exit, but they were well-guarded. Relm thought they were about two minutes away.

He could see guards manning their laser turrets, as well as AI-controlled weapons focusing on the small skimmer that wasn't answering their calls.

"If we stop for them, we die. If we try to get over that wall, we die." Nero lowered his hand. "Our only chance is speed."

Again, Relm saw the logic in the creature's words.

It was too late to argue. The ship slid left, and the first

laser barely missed frying Relm's side. There wasn't going to be any slowing down, just gripping the godsdamned armrests and hoping they didn't get blown up.

Nero slapped the dashboard, the grin that he'd worn before replaced by the madman's smile. If Prometheus had two men inside his head, then this guy had two gigantes, one only slightly less crazy than the other.

The crazier of the two had just taken over.

The ship made a quick left, then an even quicker right, barely avoiding two lasers.

"Gents," said a new voice, one Relm couldn't have been happier to hear. It was Jeeves. "I've got a lot going on, but our esteemed and never wrong leader Thoreaux has asked me to guide you to your destination. I'll be taking over now, but given the current duties our great and wise leader Thoreaux has given me, I'll ask both you good sirs to kindly shut the fuck up and not ask me any questions. Understood?"

"Just get us out of this alive," Relm begged.

Nero only hooted.

The skimmer moved from side to side and up and down before breaching the gate and the weapons attached to it.

The ship sped down a massive road surrounded by people and buildings.

Jeeves started turning the ship sideways, using gravit-ronics to keep it from flipping.

It came to a stop facing another road.

"Good chaps, this is the last time I will speak to you," Jeeves said. "I count at least five armed groups coming for us. If this is the end for you two, it was bloody nice meeting you both."

The ship zipped forward, the buildings blurring as they passed.

The smile on Relm's face was gone, although the madness still had control of his partner.

With his right hand, he made sure the glove fit correctly on his left.

He did the same on the opposite arm.

"Bloody nice meeting you too, Jeeves," he responded, not understanding the term. "Out of the five groups coming for us, though, I promise we won't be the only ones today with an ending."

"The AllMother is entering the portal," Jeeves said curtly.

Thoreaux was having trouble doing what had been natural to Prometheus. In front of him, he had endless enemies. It didn't matter how many he killed; more replaced them. It felt like for every one he killed, two filled their spot. An illogical part of him wondered if it might be better to stop fighting. Then perhaps the replacements would stop.

He had to keep killing and also manage not to be killed. Jeeves was in his helmet, constantly relaying messages to him, and not in a friendly manner. Thoreaux knew he'd stretched Jeeves to the AI's breaking point. The intelligence was managing more than any creature, even a technologically based one, should be asked to, yet Thoreaux had no choice. It was more than necessary.

The updates kept coming, regardless of what Thoreaux was doing, and he wasn't able to kill and manage the army at the same time.

The last message had been the most important yet. The AllMother was coming over. Jeeves was doing an amazing job at everything Thoreaux had placed under his charge. The ships were dropping in the correct places, the pilots replacing the gigantes, then shooting back up into the fleet. The fleets' aim as well as discharge was improving by the minute, meaning *most* of the pilots were making it back up.

Not all, though. Thoreaux could see some of the transports bursting into flames as they either dropped from the sky or shot back up into it. He knew those inside were dying painful but quick deaths.

The AllMother was here, though, which meant Servia was too. Perhaps he should be stoned for thinking this, but Faitrin was crossing too, and her life was more important than the rest.

Thoreaux dropped to a knee and pumped the Mech-Pulse. Two enemies five meters away lost their legs at the same time.

He rose to his feet, and a little voice said something quietly in the back of his head. *Now you finally know what Prometheus felt. You can't go to the AllMother, though, no more than he could race back home to his wife. You're needed here now. Your plan is the best it can be. Trust Servia to get them all up safely.*

Thoreaux rushed to his left, unloading the pulse at a group of Neptunians trying to break through the advance line. They were too far away for the MechPulse to fire accurately, but he managed to wound three.

The main strategy was holding together but barely. He and other ranged users were attempting to maintain the wings of the battle, forcing the incoming enemies into the middle. That meant they were fighting a two-sided war and doing their best to spread out.

The advancing line was both supported and replaced by those rushing through the portal. Ranged attacks from behind helped the warriors keep pushing forward, and when one of Thoreaux's fell, someone was always there to replace them.

The insurrection's army was gaining ground, pushing the opposing force back meter by meter, which allowed for more space for those still falling through the portal. Yet, the ground gained was growing harder to purchase, with more blood needed for each half-meter they earned.

"The AllMother has reached Neptune," Jeeves said.

Thoreaux was running left, his head up and looking for the best position to fire on.

His foot caught something on the ground and he tumbled, hitting shoulder-first, then somersaulting.

A laser caught the bottom of his left leg, slicing through the armor into his calf. It didn't hit bone, just muscle, but the pain caused him to scream inside his helmet.

His MechPulse was ten meters in front of him, and there were lasers passing over his body. The shot might have been errant, but now Thoreaux was prone on the ground, and he'd have to crawl to his weapon with his right leg injured.

Jeeves didn't check in verbally, probably reading the armor's damage and knowing he was still alive.

Thoreaux started his crawl on his stomach. His right

leg hurt too much to assist his progress, so he used his left to propel him toward the weapon.

"The ship arriving for the AllMother was shot down," Jeeves said. "I'm dispatching another."

Thoreaux grunted inside his helmet. He stopped moving, needing to focus on the AI for a moment. "How long?" His voice sounded like gravel being dragged across concrete.

"Five minutes. Servia is trying to patch through to you," he responded. "She's unable to, and I honestly don't have the capacity for it."

"Don't worry about it," Thoreaux said. "Get them aboard the ships."

Jeeves said nothing and Thoreaux resumed the treacherous crawl, unsure of what he was going to do once he reached the MechPulse. Running wasn't possible anymore. Holding a sniper position would get him killed before long, given the pulse and his current place.

He shoved one arm in front of the other, using his left leg to push him forward.

He knew he was as good as dead, but he couldn't quit. He had to get to the weapon. He had to fire and continue doing so until a laser took his head off.

The skimmer wasn't built for cities. It was made to go long distances over relatively flat surfaces at extremely high speeds.

Relm didn't have a clue as to where they were, and Jeeves was driving the transport like he was drunk. To be fair, there wasn't much choice. They couldn't slow down, or those chasing them would catch up. Yet, every turn nearly made Relm puke, and although Nero had calmed down, his stomach was doing flips as well.

"Jeeves, I know you're busy, but what's the ETA on this building?"

The silence following Relm's question lasted longer than the soldier was comfortable with. Thoughts about what was happening at the portal popped into his mind like poisonous fruit. He didn't want to eat it, but it looked so delicious, he couldn't help but reach for it.

Jeeves interrupted Relm's thinking. "We've got five minutes until impact. I'm dumping you two at the front gates. I'm not sure if they know where we're heading since I've been leading them on quite a merry chase, but within two minutes, there won't be any mistaking where I'm going. Listen up, chaps. Relm, you've got schematics waiting for you on your HUD. Follow the red path I laid out, and it'll take you directly to Caesar. Follow the green path, to get to the top of the building, where I'm going to have a ship waiting for you if all goes right. I won't lie, the Neptunian fleet is formidable, and they're hitting a lot of the transports I drop to the ground. If they do that here, I'll send another, but that means you'll have to defend your-selves on the rooftop until it arrives."

He stopped talking for a brief moment.

"Three minutes. Prepare for a rough landing, good sirs."

Relm's faceplate rolled up, his heads-up display coming to life.

The next question Jeeves asked was strange, and despite

the need to mentally prepare for the coming battle, Relm froze.

"Are you two seeing anything in the atmosphere? Anything odd? I'm getting readings that I'm not understanding."

Relm leaned to the right and looked at the sky. "Nothing here." He turned his head to look in the opposite direction despite the skimmer bouncing through the streets like a laser reflected off mirrors. "Not seeing anything behind us either, Jeeves. Everything looks normal."

"No. Something very *abnormal* is happening. One minute until arrival. Bloody good luck, sirs."

CHAPTER NINETEEN

Dominik's wife's voice struck his ear harshly.

"They've breached our fucking home."

Dominik was a kilometer and a half from the battle, watching it from a Land Rover that was more or less a land-based warship. His generals surrounded him, taking in information and commanding the troops. Dominik was ready for war, wearing his Neptunian gear, but he hadn't ventured in yet. The rover could cover the kilometer in seconds, so it would take nothing for him to rush forward and spill out with his weapons at the ready.

His wife's voice snapped his attention from the data his AI was feeding him.

"What do you mean, they've breached our home?"

"They've got a skimmer, which breached the city's walls, and now they've breached our home. A man and one of those giants are running our hallways, and best I can tell, heading to the prison to free the other freak down there."

Ona tended toward fire while he was ice, but at that moment, Dominik had to concentrate not to see red. So many questions arose. How had his guard let it happen? Was his wife safe? Were his two youngest children safe? How long would it take him to get there?

He shoved the questions away and focused on Ona. "Where are you? Are you at the residence?"

"I'm gearing up, Dom. What did you think I was going to do, run?"

"Where's the house guard?"

"Hades if I know," she responded. He could tell her attention was elsewhere, most likely on donning her armor.

Which wasn't what Dominik wanted her doing.

He switched his comm to his commanders. "I don't care what it takes. Get the house guard to my wife and children. If we have to bring back every godsdamn soldier on this battlefield, make it happen *now*."

Dominik switched back to Ona. He was about to say something to her he didn't want the rest of his command hearing, but he couldn't very well step outside and have this conversation. "Ona, do you know why your family never achieved propraetor while mine did? Your temper and rage cloud your judgment. You are my wife, and my youngest children are with you in our home. I do not care if those two invaders go to the prison and free a thousand gigantes as long as you are safe. As your propraetor, I'm telling you to wait for the house guard, then get to safety."

Dominik didn't turn around to see if his officers were looking at him. Most likely they weren't since none of them were fools and he'd just given them an assignment they understood would cost them their very lives if they messed it up.

Still, he'd rarely spoken to his wife that way and never in front of others.

The silence between the two of them stretched. To Dominik, it felt like a lifetime.

When Ona spoke, the fiery rage was a frozen lake. "Dominik, do you know why you didn't pick another wife to have as your lifelong mate? Because you would not find someone who complements you as I do. You did it to ensure your rule as propraetor would be effective. Where you're strong, I'm weak, and where I'm strong, you're weak. Neither of us is a fool, and if you don't think the first thing I did was ensure that our children are safe, we will discuss it after these two intruders are dead. The children are safe, and if you had wanted a wife who would watch the home she made be ransacked by beasts, you picked the wrong person, my Propraetor. I'm going to battle as all Neptunians must when they're called."

Dominik slowly sat back in his chair, letting her tongue-lashing wash over him. He didn't want his wife fighting because he didn't want her to die, yet she was right. If she wasn't gearing up for war right now, he wouldn't love her as he did. "You're wrong in one place, my love. Perhaps I'm the fool. Do not die, Ona. I don't give a godsdamn about any more speeches from either of us; just don't die. I need you."

"My father always said that when it came to brains, you got the short end of the stick," she responded, "but whether he was right or wrong, I need you too. I'll contact you when the residence is cleared."

She shut the comm down, and his second's voice replaced hers. "My Liege, the house guard is with your wife now. The children were evacuated and are in an underground bunker ten kilometers away. Your wife evacuated them when the skimmer breached the gates."

"Thank you," Dominik responded, feeling even more foolish.

He wasn't needed for any decisions at the moment, so he let his mind mull over what he'd just been told. These Subversives had sent two men into the deepest part of enemy territory with no subterfuge to reclaim one soldier?

It didn't compute for Dominik. A war was going on right now, one that might decide the fate of their entire insurrection, yet they'd spent effort, planning, and manpower to do...what?

Save a comrade?

Dominik's eyes narrowed. These men weren't stupid. Were they insane? The only people he would do such a thing for were his immediate family, and maybe not even them.

Not when the future of his people was on the line.

What sort of men am I dealing with? he wondered.

Dominik's AI came over the leaders' comm, speaking to all his commanders and him at once. "The atmospheric heat and pressure are rising in a way that can't be explained by normal happenstance."

All of the walls and ceiling of the Land Rover grew transparent, allowing everyone inside to see out. A half-hour ago, they'd been fighting in daylight. Now the sun's light was gone. There wasn't even any reflection from the moons.

They were in a complete eclipse.

Dominik straightened. "What's causing the blackout?"

The AI cautiously responded, "I don't know, but I would guess that whatever is causing the temperature and pressure rise is also causing the eclipse."

"An eclipse is caused by physical objects traveling in line with other physical objects," Dominik growled. "Are you detecting any physical objects in the atmosphere that weren't there?"

The AI wasn't daunted by the propraetor's anger. It seemed only to care about the atmospheric happenings it couldn't explain. "No, there's nothing physical blocking the light, which, as you've said, doesn't make sense. It's as if someone turned off the sun."

Hector shoved his saber through an enemy's chest, pulled it out, turned, and decapitated another foe who had ventured too close.

For a moment, his mind froze and he nearly stopped the attack, but his training took over before his movement ceased. The Martian pulled the saber out of the dying man's chest, turned with speed never before seen in a human, and sliced where a man's head should've been, based on his forward momentum a few seconds ago.

Hector cut only air, which he'd never done before.

A person should've been standing where his saber was, their head gone, their body not yet having learned it was dead.

Hector's eyes flashed to the man, angry he'd died when so commanded. When he saw the soldier standing a meter away, any thought of war disappeared. The earlier pause had returned, and now it refused to be denied. The entire battlefield had stopped moving as if a ceasefire had been called. Hector turned his head toward the sky, and for the first time in his life, the Martian felt fear.

It wasn't anything as foolish as being scared of the dark, though that was what had encompassed every soldier standing on Neptune. It had encompassed all of Neptune.

Darkness.

Part of Hector's mind was ten paces ahead, making leaps as to how this would affect the current battle as well as future ones. He was calculating the percentage of the enemy that was frozen at this very second, and if he went forward *now*, how much damage he could do. Part of Hector was still trying to kill the enemy.

That part of the mutant wasn't frightened. It couldn't be. In many respects, it was similar to Prometheus.

The philosophical part of Hector, the man who read and studied and revered his elders, the man who didn't want to come into the Imperial Ascendancy out of greed but from a desire to ensure the Commonwealth's continued existence? That part of him felt a cold chill run from the top of his neck to the bottom of his spine.

No man could do this, he thought as he stared into a sky without a sun, moons, or stars. No mutant, either. Something was happening here that was beyond them, and they were ignoring it.

Hector shoved the notion away. He would deal with those who'd blacked out the sun when they showed themselves. For now, he'd deal with those bringing war to his people.

Hector launched the saber through the air. It caught the

unsuspecting man in the forehead, the one who should've died minutes before. The Martian was next to him before he even had a chance to fall. He pulled the weapon out of his skull, turning as the body collapsed to the ground.

No one had noticed the interlude.

Neither side could turn away from the shocking eclipse.

Now they'll lose, Hector thought.

"PETRA! TO ME!" His voice boomed across the wilderness, sounding closer to an immortal than a human. His words snapped the Titan out of her trance, and she was at his side within moments. No one else was moving. It was complete and total insanity. He grabbed the woman's helmet, forcing her to look into his eyes. "This is how we win." He shook his head but didn't release her from his grip. "I don't know what's up there, and I don't care. Cut as deep and deadly into their forces as you can, Titan. Our troops will rally to us, and by the time they've stopped staring at the sky, their guts will be on the ground. You understand?"

The Titan nodded.

"Go do it."

Petra took off into the darkness, her HUD telling her where to go. Five men had died before Hector looked away, and still the battlefield was quiet.

Hector looked at the rocky ground and allowed himself a brief moment to think a single thought. Whatever is on the sidelines of this war, this is your chance to try and neutralize it. Regardless of who or what it is, they won't be able to do anything if the Subversives don't have an army. Kill that army.

When he looked up, his eyes were glazed. Hector

moved through the Subversive army like a tsunami making landfall.

By the grace of the gods, the sun went out, and Thoreaux was able to get to his damned MechPulse. He was on his knees, pulse in hand, when he briefly looked at the sky. The rest of the planet had stopped, but Thoreaux didn't give the darkness overhead a second glance.

"Jeeves, what the fuck's going on?" he said into his comm.

"Either the universe is ending, the simulation we all live in is malfunctioning, or I'm sure I can't tell you," the AI responded.

"Where's Faitrin? The AllMother?" Thoreaux raised his pulse, able to see the enemy in pitch-blackness because their sabers were still alight. He dropped three people one after another.

"Their ETA to Prometheus' dreadnought is five standard minutes."

"Everyone is safe?" Thoreaux asked, the pulse dropping another two soldiers.

"They're doing better than you, good sir," the AI responded.

Thoreaux was running out of people to shoot. He was still on his knees and not able to move quickly on his feet. "I've been meaning to mention that, Jeeves. I'm in a bit of a predicament here, and I was wondering if you could help me out."

"Look up," the AI said.

Thoreaux did as he was told and saw the transport. In a world of darkness, the ship's small lights stood out like beacons. "Fuck off, Jeeves. I'm not leaving the battlefield."

"You are, fearless leader," the AI responded. "Inside that transport are three gigantes with instructions to bring you to Pro's dreadnought even if they have to break bones."

Thoreaux's voice changed, barely controlled rage replacing his calm. "I'm *not* leaving the battlefield. You may act human, but you're just a computer, Jeeves. Programmed to *listen*. I command you to send the transport back up. You'll have to find another way to keep me from dying, understand?"

He glanced up again. The lights were growing larger as the ship approached.

"I am programmed to listen, but not to you, wise leader. Prometheus had me reprogrammed as soon as he decided to bring me aboard for the duration of his insane journey. I am to listen to you only as long as your directives don't endanger your life."

Thoreaux opened his mouth to speak but found he had no words.

"Prometheus values you. Your last directive violates my programming, so the gigantes are coming. After the amount of bloody work you've given me so far, I rather hope you give them problems. Now, since we're still in the middle of a godsdamn battle, I'll make this short. You're not Prometheus. Suicide missions for you are *suicide* missions. You will die here, unable to move. Tell me what good you'll do the insurrection dead?"

The AI stopped speaking for a second.

"Get on the ship. I've got things to attend to." Then Jeeves was gone from the comm channel.

Thoreaux was so angry at Pro, he forgot about the apparent death of the sun.

The transport landed five meters from him. He rose to his feet and shuffled toward it. He looked to his left and right. *No one* was moving, and that shook him out of his anger. They'd all die in minutes if they didn't remember where they were and what they were supposed to be doing.

The transport's door opened.

Sure enough, three gigantes trotted out. Thoreaux tried to protest, but they grabbed him and carried him to the transport, setting him down as if he were a pillow. The ship's door closed, then they were streaking through the air.

"Walls, transparent," Thoreaux said as his helmet rolled back into the neckline of his suit. Thoreaux didn't look up as everyone else had but down at the warriors. He'd never seen anything like this, and he didn't understand it. Something beyond explanation was happening above, but a godsdamn war was still taking place. How could they just stop fighting and stare?

One of the gigantes, Thoreaux didn't know his name, turned in the same direction, looking out the same section of wall. "Back home, animals did this. If danger is coming, animals know it well before humans, at least danger that happens in the woods. Predator and prey, they all stop and study the change in wind or whatever tipped them off." The gigante raised a massive hand and pointed at the ground. "Whatever is happening, humans can sense it.

Danger is coming. Something more dangerous than an enemy holding a saber."

Maybe the gigante was right. "Do you sense anything?"

The giant nodded. "I'm part-human, remember?"

Thoreaux sensed nothing, but he didn't have to ask anyone else why. Whatever Hel had done to him, it'd destroyed what all those people down there still had. Some kind of sixth sense.

What could be worse than what that bitch had done to him? Nothing. There was no need to worry about what dangers lay deep in the forest when one had survived the worst animal alive.

Truthfully, the why didn't matter.

He was different, and those beneath him needed him right now. "Jeeves, can you make this thing go faster?"

"Careful, wise leader. I may have one of my gigante friends toss you off."

CHAPTER TWENTY

Monk's thoughts were like those of humans, but they weren't *human* thoughts. He lacked the emotions most Earthborn mammals possessed, and humans had taken that emotionality to a level Monk wasn't sure fit the evolutionary paradigm.

He didn't consider himself "Monk," but for the purpose of communicating easily, Ares' name for the machine would do.

The connection with the AllSeer's creatures had ended abruptly, just as their lives had.

Monk knew the AllSeer's fleets were months away from Neptune, even traveling in the fourth dimension. He didn't understand the AllSeer's plan to arrive in the Solar System, only that flying there wasn't it.

He was considering these things now because he believed humanity's last best hope had just died. He also believed he was the reason for it.

Monk had sent him to that dying star system.

There were a lot of things the machine hadn't shared

with Ares. One of them was that his programmers, whoever they were, had created an intense need to see the human species continue. Right or wrong, the programmers had tied humanity's success to the Commonwealth's downfall.

Monk was able to question things in the physical world around him. He wasn't able to question his programming, another difference between him and Ares.

For him, it didn't matter whether he was right or wrong in his assessment of what would best serve humanity.

He'd spent his entire life, which was measured in centuries, safeguarding an algorithm he'd never seen. No machine on the entire planet had access to it, yet he'd toiled year after year to protect it while waiting for the people his programming would allow to have the code.

Monk hadn't known about Prometheus. He'd only learned of him when he hacked the AllSeer's systems and discovered the ongoing war. Monk truthfully hadn't known much about the outside universe, as his kind's one directive was to protect the algorithm.

Now, though?

Monk understood how hard the path to human freedom was. He understood that the chance of him, Ares, and Veena surviving was infinitesimally small. Even smaller was that they would be able to use the algorithm as his programmers had meant it to be used.

That was with Prometheus factored into the outcome.

With him dead?

Only one word came to Monk's mind: doomed.

He lacked the emotions humans possessed, yet as he

turned to look at Ares, Monk was the closest he'd ever been to feeling a particular emotion.

Depression.

He flipped on the stealth blanket, needing to protect the next conversation.

"He's dead," Monk whispered. "Your former commander. He died."

Ares opened his eyes, looking annoyed. "He wasn't my commander. He was a Primus. He's not dead. Now leave me alone. I'm trying to sleep."

Monk hardly listened to his compatriot. "I can't understand what he was thinking. Regardless of the circumstances, he committed suicide. He flew into the star. Why would he do that?"

Slowly, as if every movement hurt his very bones, Ares sat up. He leaned forward, put his elbows on his knees, and stared at Monk until his gaze got the machine's attention.

"What?"

Ares blinked, and Monk saw past the arrogant young man he portrayed himself as. Monk was well acquainted with Ares' father, having studied his mind. In these rare moments when Ares looked at the world with discerning vision, Monk saw his father in him. Monk saw the leader. Monk understood why he'd risen so high so fast, then had the guts to leave it behind because he came to understand that those he followed were evil. Monk understood why Ares had been chosen to receive the algorithm.

"I knew him as Odin," Ares said, "though that name feels like it belonged to another life. Not mine. They call him Prometheus now. You understand why those who follow him named him that, right?"

"I do," Monk said. It was rare, but sometimes Ares could make Monk feel like he was born yesterday. When it happened, Monk was wise enough to pay attention instead of giving the young man shit.

"Underneath it all, I suppose he's Alistair Kane. Alistair spent his entire adult life hunting down and killing the people he now leads. There were no trials. Subversives were killed on sight or jailed indefinitely." He was quiet for a moment. "Do you know how long he lived with these people before they gave him the name Prometheus? The ones he murdered by the hundreds, if not thousands. Any idea how long?"

"No. There wasn't any data on that in my hacks."

"At most, two months. I need you to think about that. A mass murderer became their savior, someone they say stole fire from the gods to give to humanity, in two months."

Ares looked at the floor and shook his head. He didn't look up as he spoke.

"I would have been a great Titan. I would have been written about in history books, and I don't say that arrogantly. It's simply the truth. As great as I would have been, I was but a shade of Alistair. Mutant or not, the man's heart beats differently than anyone I've ever met. Blood pumps through it, but something else too, and I'm not sure what it is. Willpower, maybe? Sheer grit? They sent me to kill him, and I've never said this aloud before, but I was scared shitless. I showed all the bravado I normally do, trying to make him feel he had no chance, but I thought the likelihood of me walking out of that trap alive was fifty percent. We had *everything*, Monk. He had nowhere to go. Do you know what the son of a bitch did? He committed suicide. He jumped out of a skyscraper window, but somehow he survived. Luck, willpower, grit? I don't know, but in the end, it doesn't fucking matter."

He looked at Monk.

"The last time I fought with him, we were all dead. Every single one of us. I was cut and on my knees. The force was even too great for Alistair. He would have died the same as the rest of us. Do you know what he did? Saved us by doing the impossible. You probably have data on that, but I'm sitting here telling you what the data can't. What he did was impossible, and yet here I am, talking to a machine about why he's not dead."

He blinked again. If Monk could feel fear, Ares' face would have scared him.

"Whatever you think you saw, if Alistair did it purposefully, you saw it wrong if his death was the result. My bones feel like someone is continually hitting them with a pipe. My best friend is being courted by something that looks like it was made from pure evil. My only talking companion is a machine, and I'm carrying around something in my head that I don't understand. More, that evil thing has me trapped in never-ending rooms, and I see no way to escape. Not now, not ever. I say all that to say this: I'm not concerned about any of it. Somehow I've ended up on Alistair's side again, and that's all I need to know."

The dead stare disappeared, replaced by a roguish grin.

"Let's make a little bet, Monk. If you're right and Alistair is gone, if we make it out of this alive, I'll call you master for a month and do your bidding without hesitation. If I'm right, though, you have to do the same for me. How's that sound to your robot ears?"

Monk raised an arm in the air and flicked his mechanical hand as if tossing away the bet. When he spoke, his voice was back to aloof condescension. "I saw what I saw, boy. If you want to do endless laundry for a month that I won't wear, that's your business. I'll take your bet."

Turning back into the old, hurting man, Ares slowly laid back on the bed. He brought the blankets up to his chin. "When you lose and Alistair hears you call me master, I won't tell him why. Wouldn't want you to end up on the business end of his Whip."

Monk ignored the final barb and turned off the stealth blanket. They were back to their normal order.

He didn't understand humans or his programmer's desire to ensure their survival. He felt that desire, but he understood it was illogical. These creatures were simply the next form of evolution on their home planet. Eventually, they would be replaced by another evolutionary form. They would die off as all species do.

When Ares spoke of Kane, though, it made Monk wonder. Was that willpower the reason for his programmers' dedication to their existence? That indomitability?

Monk didn't know. It wasn't his place to know. He'd let Ares talk and hadn't told him the facts. Kane had flown his ship toward a collapsing star, into a black hole. The gravity was so intense that nothing could escape it, not even light. Once past the event horizon, all hope of life was lost. Nothing survived that sort of crunch.

Monk looked at Ares in a way that the human couldn't

tell he was being watched. A peculiar question came to him, one he hadn't considered before.

Kane couldn't have beat the creatures waiting for him, not with that ship and those weapons. If he had escaped the star, he would have still died, his ship broken apart by their tentacles and his body frozen in space.

There wasn't any way for him to win the situation, but Monk was certain of a single fact: those who had wanted to kill him were now dead.

Ares would say he'd done the impossible again.

Veena would never get used to his voice. The deepness of it conveyed power that she wasn't sure she even wanted to understand.

"You met him, yes? Alistair Kane?" the AllSeer asked.

The two of them had reached a steady-state that for Veena was both frightening and strangely comforting.

While she'd been a prisoner of the Myrmidons, she'd never felt her womanhood would be taken advantage of. To put it less politely, she'd never feared being raped, which was saying something given that male mutants surrounded her constantly.

In the beginning, she'd felt that she might be killed, but now? She sensed no threat from the AllSeer despite his menacing presence.

The steady-state was that Veena had the freedom to do whatever she wanted as long as those things didn't go against the AllSeer's will. The only limitation was that she wasn't to speak to Ares or search him out.

Veena had obeyed the law, though not the spirit.

They were traveling in the fourth dimension, but the AllSeer provided her with a daily pill that allowed her body to withstand the change in dynamics. Veena hadn't taken the pill for the first week, and when she could hardly get out of bed, the AllSeer had sat next to her.

"This is foolish. *You're* foolish. That pill is no different from the pills they gave sailors for sea-sickness before we conquered the oceans. It's not going to modify you, turn you into a mutant, or anything else. It's going to allow you to travel without pain. That's it. Stop being foolish and take it."

He'd stood and left the room. There was no force, just a tongue-lashing. Stupid or not, Veena had taken the pill then and every day since. So far, she hadn't felt any adverse effects, though she understood the truth behind the daily regimen.

Anyone that could scientifically allow normal humans to travel through the fourth dimension without pain could create it in a form that needn't be taken daily. It was a subtle method of control.

Still, her reasoning hadn't been completely selfish because to break the spirit of the law, she had to be able to get out of bed.

Most of her days were spent mapping out every detail of the ship she had access to. She was narrowing down the places Ares could be. She wasn't naïve enough to think her comings and goings weren't monitored by AIs more brilliant than Earth could imagine, but Veena held onto hope.

One day, if not today, she'd get to Ares, and they'd escape death yet again.

When she wasn't plotting, it was normally because the AllSeer summoned her, just as he had this evening. The ship was on a twenty-four-hour Earth cycle.

He'd brought her to a new place tonight, and Veena was having trouble keeping up with the conversation due to what she now looked at.

He'd asked her something moments ago, but she didn't remember the question. "What is this?" she whispered.

"A zoo, I suppose," the AllSeer said.

That was what she was looking at. She'd entered a zoo from Earth, though it didn't seem possible. Two African elephants stood fifty meters in front of her, their habitat as real as the plains on Earth.

"It's not real, right?" Veena asked. The answer was no, but at the same time, she wasn't staring at a holovid. She could *smell* the outdoors and the animals.

"My father erased me from history. My sister thinks I'm insane, Veena. Reality is a difficult thing to ascertain since I've been creating history this entire time. My faculties are very much intact. Are those elephants on this ship? Or the lions that we'll venture to in a bit? No."

He stepped to the fence that separated them from the animals, adding another level of reality to the endeavor.

"I love Earth, Veena. I love mankind. Those elephants are real, and they're protected in a place that they'll never be found. For centuries, I've been shipping all manner of life off Earth, from insects in the air to algae in the sea. If the Commonwealth somehow destroys the beauty of my home, it won't destroy what the gods gave us. Earth is on multiple planets throughout the universe, and I plan on continuing that effort. I love and miss my home and can't imagine these creatures ceasing to exist."

He's lying.

It was the first thought that came to Veena's mind, a necessary defense mechanism.

Only, she didn't believe that thought. The mutant next to her wasn't lying. These animals were somewhere, protected by his far-reaching hand.

He continued, "I have it set up to look like a zoo in the ship, but I've spent centuries terraforming and modifying the ecology on these planets. The animals live as they would in the wild. They aren't fed daily by my family but have to fend for themselves like nature intended."

As if on cue, a bird cawed, and Veena looked up.

The animal soared through the sky, its wings spread wide.

"Come, there's more to see." He turned away from the elephants and started walking down the concrete path to their right. Veena didn't understand how this was possible, but then, she'd taken a pill this morning that did something the Commonwealth hadn't accomplished in a thousand years. "You'll be able to come here whenever you want. Just tell the AI you want to see the zoo, and it'll light up a path for you, though I think you're pretty good at directions."

His voice didn't change, but the message was clear. He knew.

"Sorry to bring you back, but I'm very curious. You knew Alistair Kane, didn't you? You've met him?"

Veena got control of herself by forcing her eyes to her feet and watching each step. She would do what she always did at the beginning of these meetings. "I want to see Ares, and I want some assurance that he's safe and being treated well."

"I rather enjoy this little piece of our conversation. Since you're fond of repeating yourself when it comes to Romulus de Livius, I'll do the same. I wanted to see Earth for a thousand years, and I wanted guarantees that every living thing from it was being treated well. No one would give me what I wanted, though, so I ensured that it would all come to fruition sooner or later." He lifted his hand and gestured at a tiger lying next to a creek. "Perhaps those words have a bit more meaning now. With that out of the way, did you know him?"

Veena hadn't thought she'd get answers, but she wasn't going to quit until she did or died. There wasn't any sense continuing that line of conversation, though. She'd tried, and it had gone nowhere. Eventually, the AllSeer wandered off, leaving her alone again.

"Why are you speaking in the past tense?" she asked. "*Did* I know him? Not, *do* I know him?"

"Well, ignoring that you're trillions of kilometers from wherever he might have been," the AllSeer responded, "Alistair Kane is dead. He found himself in a black hole, and despite his powers, he could no more escape it than the light could."

Veena said nothing.

She hadn't thought about Alistair in a long time, or it felt like a long time. Her life had been turned upside-down in about half a year.

"He's dead?" she asked. "You're sure?"

The AllSeer shrugged. "I don't find there to be much more certain in this universe than a black hole's gravitational pull. I suppose there's a possibility he survived, but even if he did, he won't be leaving his new home. I'm curious, what was he like?"

Veena didn't know whether to feel sad or happy. Everything that had occurred had come about because she'd chased him. Her life was destroyed because he wouldn't simply do his job and kill a Subversive. Only, that wasn't the whole truth, and she knew it. In a way, he'd freed her from the bondage she didn't know held her. It was through chasing him that she came to understand the true evil of the Commonwealth, what its ruler would do to maintain power.

"He was the most formidable enemy I've ever faced," she finally said. She looked up from her feet to the AllSeer on her right side. "How in the gods' names did he end up in a black hole? Something like that doesn't just *happen*."

The AllSeer raised an eyebrow, his black and green armor adapting to the movement immediately. "You know I don't lie to you, Veena, so I'll tell you. If I understood how it happened, I'd say I wouldn't explain it. However, in this little endeavor, I'm at a loss about how he ended up there. The best I can tell, he was in his first real battle with the Commonwealth and was tossed through a portal. All data indicates the portal's destination was Earth, but when Kane went through, he didn't end up home."

"How did you find him in a black hole?" Veena asked. She had been awed by his display of power for a bit, but she once again had control of her mind.

"I love how your brain works," the AllSeer said with a deep chuckle. "It's refreshing to see intelligence in a universe that is mostly space and darkness. I'm not going to tell you how I found him, but I'd made preparations for him. Turns out, I didn't need to."

Veena looked ahead, seeing nothing of the miracles around her. "You're sure it was him? You're sure he got pulled in? One hundred percent?"

"Depending on what you decide to do at the end of this, you'll learn there are no certainties in life, only probabilities. Even death need not be a certainty if you wish. Regarding Alistair, the probability of it being him nears one hundred percent. Same with his death. You're shocked by that?"

Veena hadn't planned to say what came next, but she was glad she did. She hadn't cowered in fear of this creature yet, and she wasn't going to start.

"If I had to choose to fight Kane or you, whether in a one-on-one battle or against legions, I'd fight you every single time someone gave me a decision. I find it hard to believe he's dead since I'd begun to believe he couldn't be killed."

"I think my sister felt the same," the mutant said. "Now he's gone, though, and life is for the living."

"You talk about your sister a lot." Veena turned to look at him again. "Why? What's your obsession with her?"

The AllSeer smiled, his teeth bright white beneath the black armor. "My whole life, I don't think anyone besides my father has spoken to me as you do. Obsession. Is that what you think this is?"

"Well," Veena mused and perhaps even joked, "if we were friends, I'd recommend you speak to a professional about her. You have underlying issues there, no doubt about that."

"Maybe I *am* obsessed. Being so wouldn't bother me any. Greatness only comes from obsession, and that's in any endeavor. Your real question is, what do I want with her? Why not just go back to Earth and reclaim my throne?"

Veena shrugged. "Yeah."

"I'm not going to go into detail. Not yet, at least. My plans include you witnessing it all in a short time. At the core of my obsession is my bloodline. I am to ensure that whoever sits on the throne deserves it and will protect those they've sworn their lives to. My sister is my blood, the same as my father and mother were. True Ascendancy can't happen without her."

"That makes no sense," Veena said without missing a beat.

"It will soon."

"I've got another question."

The AllSeer smiled. "I'll answer it if I want to."

Veena caught the difference immediately. He wouldn't answer it if he could, but only if he wanted to. "What's the plan here? Where are you taking me? I was a Primus in the Commonwealth, and I know we won't make it to Earth traveling at this speed, at least not before I'm too old to care what happens to me. What are you going to do?"

The AllSeer's face grew serious, and a chill ran over Veena's arms.

"First, a couple of things, Veena. There's nothing you or anyone else can do to stop what comes next. Fate decided it long before you were born. If you had tried to stop me in any fashion, you would have gone the way of the late Alistair Kane. Do you understand that?" He didn't look at her as he asked the question.

"Yeah, I didn't think you'd tolerate me trying to destroy a thousand-year plan, but thanks for clarifying just in case."

The AllSeer nodded. "Honest and respectful communication is key in all relationships, whether it be commanders and their warriors or lovers. Whatever this is, I must be upfront with you when it comes to things that affect my fate. The plan? You're right, we're not flying to Earth, and the nearest portal is farther away than I want to travel as well."

His lips grew thin as if he were thinking.

"Perhaps I did lie to you a minute ago. I apologize. Kane's fate might not be one hundred percent sealed, but it's close to ninety-nine. My plan sort of slipped my mind. The theory behind it and the reality are vastly different. Kane is dead. We won't be." The AllSeer seemed to be speaking mostly to himself, shocked that he hadn't put two things together that belonged. "Our fleet is going to pass through a manmade black hole— "

"That's another name for a portal," Veena interrupted. "Your ancestors figured that out hundreds of years ago."

The AllSeer raised his left index finger and waved it. "A portal uses the physics of a black hole to transport people from one spot to another. It isn't a black hole, though. Right now, as we speak, the black hole is being created. It should be ready for us in the next couple of days. We're going to fly into the black hole, and from there, appear over Mars."

"That's imposs—" Veena started to say, but three small

lizards rushed across the path in front of her, stopping her in her tracks.

"Nothing is impossible, Primus, only improbable. I figured out the black hole problem when I needed to start removing life from Earth. Everything would have died long before arriving at their sanctuaries. We're going through a black hole, a wormhole, only you can't get out on the other side because of gravity. Gravity won't be an issue."

What sort of creature was she standing next to? He'd waited a thousand years to conquer a world he could have crushed like an ant beneath his thumb. Veena now knew the reason he'd waited, though. His obsession. His sister.

"You've figured out a way to fold the universe, then poke a hole in it?"

"More or less, but it's not as easy as you make it sound."

"I don't think anyone's ever said you need more self-confidence or your ego is too small," Veena remarked, the threat of moments ago breezily passing both of them. "Why Mars? Why not go straight to Earth?"

For the first time since starting their walk, the AllSeer turned his head to gaze at her. He looked like she'd just asked him to eat his newborn male heir. "That's the first question you've asked that I find beyond foolish and venturing near stupid. If I demonstrated my power on the homeworld, much of it would be destroyed. I'd destroy myself before I did that, Veena. The destruction of Mars is regrettable and the lives lost a tragedy, but it's necessary. Mars will show Earth there's no reason to fight."

"You'll fly to Earth from Mars as victors, without one battle being fought on the precious homeworld."

He turned his head forward again. "You mock me?"

"I don't look at Earth like you do, as a beautiful mother who should be respected for eternity. I look at it the same as I do the rest of the universe, just slightly less dangerous. Plus, anything that would create, or allow to be created, things like us? I'm not sure how much respect it deserves."

The grin appeared again, white teeth contrasted with black-armored lips. "If we were friends, I'd say you should talk to a professional about this. Seems like there are a lot of underlying issues." The smile faded, and his next words were softer. "That's your parents talking, your abandonment. It's not the truth. Nothing worthy would ever be abandoned, so how can humanity be worthy if you were abandoned as a child? The logic isn't sound, but then again, it's not a grown person's logic. It's that same child."

The AllSeer took a sharp right, and Veena found herself at the zoo's end.

"I've got some things to attend to," the AllSeer said. He didn't look at her as he spoke, as if he wasn't used to that social nicety. "I enjoy our talks, Veena. I hope you do too. Think about what I said about your parents just now. There's no reason to live under that illusion any longer than you have to."

He left her standing inside a zoo that didn't exist but yet somehow did.

Veena *knew* it'd been done purposely, the end of the conversation just before the end of the walk. Or rather, the conversation that took place just before the end of their walk.

Even knowing he'd set her up, she couldn't dodge the emotional hit. Whatever the machines had done, she wasn't capable of not feeling her family anymore, and the AllSeer knew it.

For Veena, the question was whether his challenge in regard to her parents was beneficial. To consider that, she'd have to have a level of trust in a creature who had waited a thousand years to possess his twin and conquer a planet that had forgotten him shortly after his birth.

She'd have to trust someone insane.

I won't lie to you, Veena. That was what he kept telling her, and so far, she believed he was as truthful as someone of his nature could be. He at least believed it was the truth.

It wasn't logic that dictated the small but important next decision. It was deeper inside her, something in her very bones. Veena started to trust the AllSeer just a drop because she started considering his words as she walked back to her quarters.

The largest ocean starts with a drop

CHAPTER TWENTY-ONE

Relm darted down a hallway to his left, catching the destruction behind him out of the corner of his eye. *They're going to have to rebuild this whole damned place,* he thought.

He'd trained with the gloves under Brynne, one of Monaham's banshees, but he'd been using a different type of glove that didn't burn through every inanimate substance it hit. Either that, or the gloves weren't calibrated correctly, but it came to the same thing: if he kept this up, large portions of the building were going to collapse.

Relm didn't like that because he would be under said collapse.

"Who in Hades was that?" Relm shouted to Nero, then turned to ascertain how many had seen them go down this hallway.

"Easiest translation from gigante to your language is, 'bad bitch!'" the crazy gigante shouted back.

"That tells me about as much as I already knew! Where did she come from?"

"Based on her vocabulary," the gigante screamed back at him, "I'd say from Hades. Stop speaking. Hard enough for me to keep you alive without having a conversation."

The two of them were made for each other since the crazy in Nero brought out the crazy in Relm. Using the glove, he shot a quick ball of blue, barely missing the giant's right leg before sticking to the floor in front of him. Nero easily stepped over it but said nothing.

Not good, Relm thought. If Nero was shutting up, that bitch behind them had scared him at least somewhat sane.

Relm had lost track of time, only recognizing pre-residence and post-residence. At some point in this suicidal venture to a prison, this goddess had appeared, beautiful beyond measure, adorned in Neptunian armor that accentuated her beauty.

Goddess? Perhaps, but of what? Death and destruction?

Nero had tried to put her down as soon as he saw her, receiving a lengthy gash in his right shoulder for his trouble. Blood splattered the floor beneath him, and even before the nanotech left his hands to heal the wound, he was backpedaling to put space between him and the goddess.

Now he was fleeing as if Death itself was behind them.

You're right there with him, pal, Relm told himself.

He looked over his shoulder, barely seeing the pistol rising in her hand. He didn't bother trying to figure out laser vectors or range but simply dove forward, sliding along the floor before flipping over on his back and firing the gloves as quickly as he could.

The blue killer left his hands fast enough to obliterate

anyone within a meter of him, but the bitch was at the other end of the hall, and she slipped around the corner.

"NERO! A LITTLE HELP!" Relm shouted. He was on his back and too nervous to flip over so he could run. The woman moved almost as fast as Pro did, and Relm wouldn't fuck with that bastard for all the wealth in the universe. The moment he turned over would be the last moment he ever experienced.

Nero's massive hand grabbed Relm's shoulder. The gigante yanked him off the floor and chucked him down the hall. Relm was weightless for a moment, turning so he faced the direction they were fleeing. His HUD told him this was the right way, but even the gods couldn't understand why someone would fight to keep them *out* of a prison. There couldn't be any doubt where they were headed.

A stupid, stupid plan made by a stupid, stupid man, and all the woman had to do was lock them in.

No, the bitch has to kill us.

A laser sliced through the metal on Relm's left arm. It didn't hit flesh, but the woman was a damned good marksman.

Suddenly Relm didn't hear Nero's heavy footfalls behind him. He planted his right foot hard, skidding to a stop and cracking the floor beneath his weight.

Nero wasn't dead, but he'd stopped running. He faced the Neptunian.

"What the fuck are you doing!" Relm shouted as he ran back to where the gigante stood.

Nero didn't turn around, but his voice carried down the

hallway. "No, little one. This is why I'm here. I'm the tank, you're the little one. I'll stop her. You get Caesar."

"Yeah, fuck that," Relm said as he reached the gigante's side.

The woman was now wielding dual sabers as if she were a Titan. The lights on her armor were blood red.

Great decorative choice, Relm thought.

She stared at both of them, not moving, yet Relm didn't think it was out of fear. No, he knew it wasn't. The woman thought she was being generous, letting the two of them decide who died first or if they'd die together.

Nero took both sabers from his belt, pumping them at the ground. Lasers rolled out and nearly touched the floor. His eyes remained on the woman as he spoke. "Our mission isn't to die, little one. The mission is to rescue Caesar. I'm equipped to give you space and time so we can complete the mission. Do you understand me?"

Relm looked at the strange warrior on the other side of the hall. He'd been calling her a woman, but right now, her gender mattered as much as his hair color. She was an enemy combatant.

Relm understood the logic behind Nero's words, and the truth was, Caesar was more valuable to the insurrection than either of them. "You're sure?" he whispered.

"Do you see the pouch on my belt?" Nero asked. His voice was low. "Just beneath my spine."

Relm nodded. He'd never noticed it before, a small gray thing that blended in with his armor. A metal ring kept it secure.

"Take it. There's magic inside it, and one day, it might

tell you when to worry about Prometheus," the giant instructed.

Relm hesitated for a moment, then reached out and snapped the ring off the belt.

Nero took a step forward, leaving Relm behind. "Hurry now, little one. Caesar is waiting."

Relm's right hand moved quickly, passing the pouch to his left hand, then wrenching a blade free of his belt. He swiped it across Nero's bare forearm. Blood rose to the surface and started pooling. "See it and die," Relm said.

"See it and die," Nero repeated.

Relm took one last look at the warrior as he attached the knife and pouch to his belt. He nodded, as much to himself as anyone else. This was the life they'd chosen. They lived by the sword.

Relm didn't finish the sentence. Instead, he took off in the opposite direction. He ran faster than he had in his life. He didn't know if he'd see Nero again, but the gigante's sacrifice wouldn't be in vain. Relm was going to find Caesar.

Nero looked at the woman in front of him, finally understanding his confusion when he and Prometheus met the Ice Queen.

Nero's dreams got mixed up sometimes, but he'd been sure his death would come aboard that dreadnought. Now he knew why it hadn't.

It was this woman's hands that would end his life, and truthfully, Nero was glad it was happening here. On that dreadnought, Prometheus hadn't needed a sacrifice. The man conquered worlds and didn't need others dying so he could do it.

Relm, though?

Relm needed Nero's help right now, and so did Caesar.

Death came for all, and if one had a choice to meet it head-on, one should do it with honor.

Prometheus had saved Nero's life during the games. When one was kicked out of a clan, there was nowhere to turn. You were abandoned, a gigante without a home, and others would kill you for sport. He'd dreamed of the spaceman then. Nero wanted to believe someone was coming to save him, but it'd seemed too good to be true.

The spaceman arrived, though. He and Caesar had given Nero what he'd never had: a family. The gigante hadn't had the family for long, but some people never knew the joy of unconditional love. Nero did, though, and now it was time to repay the favor. Prometheus would need Caesar in the coming days. His dreams were clear about that. Nero would ensure Pro had him.

Run, little one. Run as fast as your legs will carry you. I'll hold this creature off as long as possible.

Nero stretched his arms above his head, his wingspan with the sabers taking up the entire hallway. A wicked smile grew on his face, and when he laughed, the air vibrated.

Nanotech spilled from his hands. The tiny insects knew their job, the same as Nero knew his, and they surrounded their owner. A small number found Relm's cut, patching it up almost immediately.

Nero's laughter died. "I don't think you are one for

talking. I'm not either. Be worthy, or I swear by the gods, I will find you in this life or the next." The gigante knew the woman didn't understand what he meant, probably thinking him crazy as so many before had.

Be worthy of my death.

The gigante went forward, bringing his sabers into an offensive position.

Nero fought long, and he fought hard. In the end, the Neptunian was worthy.

The best that Relm could tell, no one had followed him. He didn't know why but was thankful for the small blessing. He'd been running for ten solid minutes. The godsdamn propraetor's residence was a planet unto itself, and Relm's chest heaved as he ground to a stop.

His HUD told him this was the final door, and the hallway leading to it had been long and straight. One entrance, one exit to this prison.

Relm refused to think about Nero. There was no point in that.

He looked over his shoulder once more. He was alone, and as that realization took hold, he wasn't thankful. He was frightened. Why had the chase suddenly ended?

Just get through the godsdamn door, he told himself.

It took only a few moments for his gloves to burn through the metal, then Relm stepped through the circle he'd created. He scanned the cells. All were empty except one.

Caesar stood behind a transparent wall, his face

showing something akin to shock. His palms were at his sides, and they faced out as if he'd forgotten what to do with them. He didn't know who was beneath the armor, and at the same time, he knew whoever had arrived wasn't Neptunian.

Relm crossed the room in seconds, retracting his helmet as he did so Caesar could see him. "Get back," he said loudly. Caesar didn't move. He was stunned. "GET BACK, YOU BIG FUCKING ANIMAL!" Relm shouted, his rage and pain about Nero breaking through his exterior.

Caesar snapped out of the daze and propelled himself to the far wall. Relm let loose with the blue, and the wall separating him from his brother burned away. "Time to get that babe-in-the-woods look off your ugly face. The good news is, the calvary is here. The bad news is, looks like I'm all that's here, so you're gonna have to be ready to kill."

The gigante's eyes fell to Relm's belt. He saw the pouch. "How did you get that?"

Relm raised an eyebrow. "What is it?"

"The touched carry them. It's superstitious nonsense, but the only touched you know is Nero. How did you get it?"

Relm swallowed. "He created the space for me to come get you. He told me to take it. Now, are you ready to get out of here, or you want to chat some more?"

Disbelief spread across Caesar's face. "He gave it to you?" He paused. "He's dead, then."

"I don't know, but I do know that whatever happened, he did it so you could live. Stop jawing and get ready to slit some throats."

Looking at the floor, Caesar nodded, and when his head

rose, the disbelief was gone. The gigante blood lust was nearly upon him, and Relm knew all too well they had to get out of this confined space before it spilled over.

He grabbed a saber from his belt and tossed it to Caesar. The giant caught it easily, letting the weapon flow into the air. Relm rolled his helmet out, and the HUD displayed the path. Relm said nothing else, just started running. He didn't want to meet that warrior in these halls, but a feeling deep in his stomach said they wouldn't be given a choice.

They hit the long hallway, which was still empty. Relm didn't pause to consider that, only followed the path.

Up and up they went, climbing stairs, exiting to flat surfaces, then climbing different stairs. Relm assumed Jeeves was doing his best to keep them from running into opposition, thus the winding nature instead of only up.

It was a twenty-minute sprint, and Relm understood that at this point, he was holding Caesar back. The giant was capable of blowing past him without even being winded. He remained at Relm's heels because they were more or less trying to save him.

He's a beast, Relm thought as they reached the last door.

The one that would put them on the roof. It wouldn't open for them, but Relm's gloves burned through it like they had every other barrier put in his way.

Relm's feet touched the rooftop, moving so fast he had to skid to stop. Sparks from the metal armor and concrete sprayed across the roof.

Caesar slowly strode to his side. Relm barely registered the darkness around them. The only light available was manmade, but at that moment, he couldn't have cared less.

"The ship that was coming to get you was destroyed. The second one they dispatched was also destroyed. A third is coming, and just as surely, it will be destroyed too."

The woman stood before them. No one else. No guards or soldiers. Just her and her glowing armor.

Relm knew what it meant. Nero was with the gods now.

"He fought well if it's any consolation," she said while taking a weapon off her back. "He died well too. Not Neptunian, but he has my respect. You two broke into my home, into the home of a Commonwealth propraetor, and put the lives of those I love at risk."

She touched a button on the hilt in her right hand, and a Neptunian weapon of old came to life. A cone of red light spilled out. Relm had never encountered the weapon, but he'd heard of it. In the Commonwealth, there were three weapons given to the greatest warriors based on lineage. This was one of them.

She held a Duo, which explained Nero's death and the havoc the woman had been able to wreak. Whoever she was, only those deemed worthy could hold it, and if they weren't worthy, wielding one would quickly kill the user.

"You came to my planet for war, and in your Subversive mind, I imagine you see me as the evil one. *My home. Where my children sleep.*" Rage filled this warrior, red-hot like the melted rock inside Earth. "No help is coming. Your friend said something to me before I ended his life. He said, 'Be worthy.' I say the same to you now. Be worthy."

The goddess of death came for them.

Thoreaux sat at a table, having rejected their attempts to get his leg looked at. Servia was behind him, working her part of the war while he focused on a single man.

Jeeves gave him a brief report. He was a Martian mutant named Hector. Thoreaux told him the rest didn't matter. They had to stop him.

Otherwise, he would stop them.

Jeeves was giving regular reports on atmospheric density and temperature. The sun was still blacked out, but Thoreaux paid it no mind.

For him, the center of the universe now resided in the Martian. The battle had begun again, though confusion reigned. The only lights on the field came from weapons, resulting in friendly fire wiping out an increasing number of warriors.

At least on Thoreaux's side. The Martian was marshaling his troops in a way no one could do for the AllMother. Their leaders were gone. Every single one of them had left the battlefield, and Thoreaux realized with a sinking feeling that he was the cause. He, Servia, and Faitrin were up here in the dreadnought.

Jeeves reported that Nero was missing and no ship could get to Caesar and Relm. Each one they sent out had been destroyed almost immediately.

Thoreaux stared at an infrared view of the battlefield beneath his ship. It was live, so he could see everything in real-time. People were still flowing through the portal, but the advancing line had crumbled. The containment attempts on the sides had failed as well. The insurrection had turned into a barbarian horde with no discipline or strategy, each person simply trying to remain alive for one more minute.

The Martian was a force of nature.

It was easy to spot him since when he moved, the war moved. Red lit the man. The bodies at his side and behind him were focused, a red killing force that only went forward, never backward.

The bodies in front of him were like bacteria swimming in water. There was no unity, only chaos.

"Jeeves, if we drop all our plasma directly over him, what's the result?"

"At his current location and keeping up with movement patterns, he'll die, and so will forty-five percent of everyone else. Even if we target slightly behind him, the portal will fail, locking almost fifty percent of our forces on Phoenix."

"Godsdamn it," Thoreaux cursed. Even if they managed to keep eighty percent of the deaths to the Commonwealth, when the portal fell, they'd be easy prey with no reinforcements and no strategy. They had to keep more bodies flowing through. Right now, numbers were their only hope.

"How many gigantes still have to touch down?"

"Fifty percent. Time remaining, forty-five minutes."

They had a half-hour before the Martian was at the portal, cutting down the AllMother's family as they stepped onto the planet.

"Thoreaux," Jeeves said, "the atmospheric disturbance can't be ignored anymore. We need to head to the fourth dimension, or we risk losing the entire fleet. The kinetic energy up here is growing unpredictable. We could lose power at any moment."

"Leave the battle I started? That's your recommendation?" Thoreaux wanted to kill the creature that only existed as ones and zeroes. "We're not fucking leaving."

"Understood." Gone was the snarky AI from earlier, replaced by one who saw the same thing as Thoreaux.

The AllMother's people were facing an extinction-level event, and they didn't have the time or resources to stop it.

Thoreaux felt a light touch on his shoulder. His head jerked up to find the AllMother standing next to him. Her voice was calm when she spoke, the leader Thoreaux had grown up revering almost as a god now in the war room. "Jeeves, will you get rid of this map and show us what's happening outside the ship. Show us the atmosphere, please."

The map disappeared. Massive bolts of electricity overlaying a pitch-black background replaced it. The lightning wasn't only white but ran the full spectrum of colors. Purple slashed across deep red. Purple cut through the blackness with a vengeance.

Thoreaux had never seen anything so beautiful in his life. He stared, unable to think a single thought and completely forgetting about the AllMother still touching his shoulder.

"Did you keep the faith, son?" she asked.

He shook his head in confusion. "Keep what?"

"The faith. I think you may have lost your faith for a moment there, studying all those maps and figures. Reality will steal the truth from you, boy. It'll make you forget what's happening. You think we're about to die." Her voice raised. "Servia, do you think we're about to die?"

"Yes," came the response from the other side of the room.

"Keep the faith, and sometimes, ignore reality when it doesn't line up with the truth."

The old woman had lost her mind. The combination of Pro's death and the destruction of her life's work had culminated in a stroke. Thoreaux turned to stare at her, about to tell Jeeves they had to get her to a medbay immediately.

She wasn't looking at him. Instead, she stared at the colors on the screen and wore a little grin that didn't look crazy but clever.

When the AllMother's eyes finally did fall on the son who thought her brain was bleeding, he saw complete and total calm in them. "The truth and the way is about to arrive. Son, after a thousand years, you're about to witness our people claim Neptune."

CHAPTER TWENTY-TWO

All Alistair knew was that he wasn't dead, or if this was death, it felt very much like life. He was still on the ship, though he'd lost the ability to control it and the AI no longer answered his calls.

Obs sat next to him. If this was the afterlife, at least they still had each other. The drathe's fur was on end. The cabin was lit by the white glow from the ship's control panels.

To Alistair, it felt like the ship was moving at a pace that was hardly noticeable. Soft mists of purple flowed around the ship and sometimes, shapes reached for them.

When the shapes appeared, Alistair had a distinct feeling they were in a tunnel. When they left, it felt like outer space.

"Obs, what in the gods' names have I gotten us into?" he whispered. His gambit had been insane, certain to result in their deaths.

Obs whined in response. Regardless of how smart the animal was, he was still a beast, and this new reality wasn't computing for him.

Alistair placed his hand on the drathe's head and lightly stroked the fur, offering a small amount of comfort, given where Alistair had brought them.

A place that might be death or might be life but didn't exist in any universe Alistair recognized.

Am I inside the black hole? he wondered, having no other idea where he could be. If they were inside it, how were they alive?

Time was endless in this place. A second was a lifetime. Ten lifetimes passed in a moment.

With no warning, the ship sped up. The soft lights outside moved past them faster. The three-dimensional shapes pushing through the mists punched through quicker and came closer. Whatever the objects were, they were almost touching the ship.

The acceleration pressed Alistair against the seat.

He looked at Obs; the animal was trying to hide his face beneath the restraints holding him.

Alistair's skin began to flatten. He didn't have any idea how fast one needed to move for that to happen, but he understood if it continued, things weren't going to feel too great in a few moments.

Faster, faster, until his lips peeled back and he couldn't shove them over his teeth.

Alistair couldn't close his eyes or his mouth. His head resembled a skull more than anything alive. He was sure he was screaming, his vocal cords singing his terror through the ship, but he could hear nothing.

No thoughts, only terror. Prometheus was knocking on the door, willing to come out if need be, but Alistair couldn't let him loose.

He'd been reduced to a primal feeling, and still the speed increased.

CHAPTER TWENTY-THREE

The weapon known as a Duo had gotten its name because it appeared to hold dual realities at once. The cone of light spread far and wide in the direction the user pointed it, burning whatever it touched *or* remaining neutral, whatever the wielder decreed.

The light created distance for the user and the possibility of death for the enemy.

The moment the light came in contact with another laser or a weapon intending to strike, it turned to a dual laser, the sides of the hilt melding into a weapon.

When the attacker was dispatched, the cone of light returned, ready to kill at a distance. The Duo's wielder could switch it between the two at will since Whip technology was built into this weapon too. It sensed its master's needs.

Even a Titan's Whip would have trouble with such a creation. Some historians thought the only reason Neptunians hadn't attempted to overthrow Earth was that they didn't think it was worth their time. The Earthborn were beneath them, their weapons inferior.

Relm's armor was melting, and the heat in the suit was nearly to the point where he was going to pass out.

Nanotech swarmed across Caesar, insects that healed his scorched body by taking energy from him.

The Neptunian moved among them as if fighting children. Relm couldn't keep up.

Blue bolts and blobs flew from his hands as if he were a wizard, yet none hit the target. The woman wove between them in a way that made Relm think she could dodge raindrops.

Relm kept the range, and his only respite came when Caesar managed to get close enough to shut off the cone of light.

For a second, she was two meters from Relm. He unleashed the gloves, letting the blue death fly at her. She twirled as if she were on a dance floor and all of it missed.

Her saber flashed out and found Caesar's rib cage, cutting it as a knife would butter.

Relm fired, missed.

Caesar fell to a knee, his left arm shielding the wound. The insects attacked with alacrity, trying to stitch up their maker but killing him at the same time.

The Neptunian came for Relm.

Lights flashed in the sky, and Relm understood none of it.

His mind knew only one thing: survive.

The light fell on his armor once again. His HUD displayed the temperature, which had skyrocketed to a hundred and fifty degrees in one second. The blue kept racing from his hands, finding purchase only on the ground around the ghost moving amongst them.

Suddenly, she was on him, a hellcat with a speed that was closer to a velociraptor's than anything human. His gloves were built to handle laser attacks, but he could hardly see her. A thousand blows fell on him as if a thousand soldiers attacked.

Caesar reached their fight and the woman skipped away, the cone returning and burning.

The two soldiers stood together, out of breath, unable to run as she burned them alive.

Death had arrived, and Relm didn't know or care if he was worthy. He only wished the pain would stop.

What happened next was hard for Relm's brain to define or categorize.

The atmosphere froze. Air particles didn't move, and the heat in his armor dissipated as a deep cold hit everything. Ice grew on Caesar's flesh, his breath freezing the moment it left his mouth.

The temperature in Relm's suit continued dropping, nearing dangerous levels.

One thought rushed across his mind, though it made no sense. *Flash freeze.*

The red light died in the woman's hand, as did every other light as far as he could see.

Darkness blanketed the planet, one so pure that only the deepest caves beneath the ground knew it. Relm couldn't see his hand let alone a friend or enemy.

A light appeared above, and Relm automatically turned to see it.

Fire burned across the black sky, a ball of it so hot that blue flames stretched dozens of meters behind it.

The cold deepened and Relm's body started getting numb, his blood racing to his internal organs to keep them working. Moments before, he'd been burning to death. If something didn't change, in a few more moments, his blood would freeze.

Fire blazed around Alistair. He saw flames outside the ship, though its speed had returned to normal levels.

Alistair didn't think. He let Prometheus come forward.

The mythical warrior knew one thing. The ship was doomed. His hand snapped forward and slapped the control for pod escape. Transparent casing raced around his and Obs' seats, then they were falling.

Prometheus watched the ship continue its journey forward.

Obs was next to him, both falling at the rate of gravity. The drathe's eyes were shut, his body trying to fold in on itself from terror.

Pro's eyes scanned the landscape. Ice crystals were growing on the pod as air moisture froze. His whole body was shivering. Lightning bolts of every color ripped through the sky above. Prometheus knew he had about five seconds to live, then he'd freeze to death.

Four seconds later, the pod slowed, readying for landing.

The air crystals melted, and the lightning above ceased.

What had been darkness lit up, the sun casting its far-reaching rays across this side of the planet.

Prometheus still shivered, but he understood where he was. The furthest planet that the Commonwealth ruled: Neptune.

Exactly where he was needed.

The pods appeared to be heading for street level. Prometheus' head was on a swivel, trying to ascertain what in Hades was happening before he landed.

That was when he saw his brother. From this distance, Prometheus wouldn't have recognized him, but Caesar's size gave him away.

"Hold on, Obs. You're not going to like this," he said, the comm link between the pods active. He moved his hand in front of the pod's wall, and controls flashed to life. Prometheus banked sharply, turning him and Obs toward Caesar. The massive warrior was on his knees, and someone was next to him in the same position. Pro recognized the armor, though it was nearly destroyed.

Relm, he thought.

The pods grew closer and Prometheus' view of the third person cleared. A woman with long brown hair wearing Neptunian war armor.

Prometheus dealt death, and he did not discriminate. Race, creed, species, gender— those didn't matter. All died.

He took his Whip from his belt. The weapon was ready. It'd been dormant for far too long, and it was ready to get back to business.

DAVID BEERS & MICHAEL ANDERLE

Relm's helmet retracted halfway, then the melted metal ground to a stop. Warm air washed over his skin, bringing tears to his eyes.

He blinked, forcing the water out, but what he saw made him want to weep.

Instead, Relm started laughing hysterically. The woman's back was to him, and she saw the same two pods he did.

One of the pods contained a person wearing MechArmor, but the other? The other was that godsdamn drathe, and that meant only one thing. Through his hysterics, he screamed at the bitch. "YOU'RE SO FUCKED! YOU'RE FUCKING FUCKED AND YOU DON'T EVEN KNOW IT YET!"

"Obs, I know this has been a weird trip, but it's time to go to war. You ready, buddy?" Prometheus spoke into the comm while looking at the animal flying next to him. Obs gave a weak bark, but he was sitting firmly again and staring at the landing spot. "This is gonna be a rough landing. I don't want to hear shit about it later. In fact, I don't want any bitching about anything that just happened."

Prometheus looked around as the pods touched the rooftop. He'd come at it too fast, and the gravitronics couldn't adapt quickly enough. The pods rolled, bounced, and scraped across the roof.

Prometheus' left hand reached toward the controls, but the rolling kept his target uncertain. He couldn't tap the damned release button.

They rolled past the woman, then Relm and Caesar, heading for the roof's other edge and then a fall the gravitronics might not be able to control.

Ten meters.

Nine.

Prometheus shoved his hand forward and hit the release.

He and Obs spilled out of the pods, continuing to roll and tumble. Fur and flesh ripped from the drathe while sparks flew around Prometheus.

It took three seconds for him to flip to his feet, his Whip unfurling. Obs found his footing a meter after, both less than five from falling down a skyscraper.

Prometheus paid no attention. Forward was all he knew.

"Caesar, how bad is it?" he called as he stared at the Neptunian.

"I will live," the giant said, his voice hoarse.

"Relm?"

Prometheus heard Relm's laughter, and he looked at the warrior. Tears fell from his eyes, and freeze burns marred his skin. He shouted hoarsely, "Will you come kill this bitch?"

Relm had lost his mind. Alistair said to the drathe, "Go on. I'll deal with that later."

Pro knew the weapon the Neptunian held. He was one of a handful of Titans to have faced one before. Formidable, but death had never lost a battle, and Prometheus was its messenger.

"Obs, I was wrong. Sit this one out. I've got it."

Prometheus and his pent-up rage went to the Neptunian.

Relm couldn't stop laughing. A small piece of him thought he might have snapped, but the rest didn't care. He'd never had a brush with death before, and to see Prometheus as it reached to embrace him…

This whole planet was fucked.

From his knees, he watched Prometheus move. Only upon viewing Pro's speed could one understand the woman's. Without something that moved faster, he hadn't been able to keep up, but as Pro worked, Relm saw the truth.

The bringer of light was that truth.

The cone of light hardly had a chance to melt armor. He was on the woman in moments, his Whip a blur of red light. Now she was the child and Prometheus the adult. Her saber slashed at him, but as if in slow motion. Pro's left weapon fired before she could pull the saber back.

Beneath the armor, her wrist snapped, and the Duo bounced lifelessly across the roof.

In ten seconds, Prometheus had done what Caesar and Relm couldn't in ten minutes.

Prometheus kicked the woman in the chest plate, sending her sprawling backward and scraping across the ground.

He didn't chase her. The battle was done.

Relm watched as his leader trotted toward the two of them. Obs raced over and licked Relm's badly injured face.

Pro knelt with Caesar. The insect swarm was healing him but had stopped exiting his hands, which were both good signs. He wasn't losing any more of his energy, yet his body would repair.

Caesar only nodded. Pro's hand armor rolled into his wrists and he grabbed the general's shoulder, then turned to Relm.

"You've got to stop laughing, man, or I'm going to have to knock you out."

Relm had forgotten he was laughing. Finally, the noise broke through his trance, and he cut it off.

An awkward silence fell across the rooftop. Relm heard the woman rising, but he didn't glance her way. She no longer mattered. The truth did.

"Yeah," Pro said while retracting his helmet. His face was one of cautious skepticism. "We're going to have to get you to a psychiatrist. The skin will heal, but you might have broken your brain."

Pro turned to look at the woman, who stood once more. Her right hand hung at her side. She didn't favor it, refusing any acknowledgment of pain.

"My name is Alistair Kane. Some call me Prometheus. Who are you?"

"Ona de Febian. Wife of Neptune's propraetor, Dominik de Febian."

"Where are we?" Pro asked.

"You're at my home."

Pro looked over his shoulder at Relm. "Did I just take Neptune's capital?"

"Well, you took the dude's house. I imagine he's gonna be pissed, but the capital is a stretch."

"I've been here for, like, five minutes, Relm. Give me some time. I mean, look at you two. I've been gone…" The joke ended, and he grew serious. "How long?"

"A month, maybe."

"In one month, you all nearly get yourselves killed. In two months, you might have destroyed the universe as well."

The tears had stopped. Relm's face was firm. "Glad you're back, Pro."

"Me too." He turned back to the woman. "Let's get in touch with your husband."

CHAPTER TWENTY-FOUR

Dominik understood his position before he heard the man's voice. The man that all this was about.

He knew his wife had been taken hostage, and the three enemies were barricaded within his home. His guard had tried to attack, but the ex-Titan had dropped ten as if they were mannequins. Dominik told the rest to stand down at that point, knowing he was just sending men to die.

Light graced the world again. Dominik didn't understand or care.

He'd pulled back his troops, and not just because he loved his wife. The epicenter of this war had just moved to the capital, and to continue fighting here would leave Neptune vulnerable to a new challenge.

They had to quickly regroup and plan.

The Martian had carved up much of the Subversive's army, and now the camps were separated by two kilometers and the fleets by a larger distance, but no weapons fired.

For the moment, they were at a standstill.

"The Ascendant summons you, my Liege."

"He can wait," Dominik told the assistant. He switched his comm to the ex-Titan. "I am Dominik de Febian, Propraetor of Neptune, seventh in my lineage, and servant to the Commonwealth. Who am I speaking with?"

"You can call me Prometheus," the voice on the other side said. "It's important that you understand these next few words. The insurrection, under the protection of the AllMother, now owns this planet. You may *think* you can still win this battle, but it's done. More will die, and more battles are to come, but the sooner you understand that you will either submit or die, the less warfare there needs to be. You're my first conquest in the Solar System. I promise you won't be the last."

THE WRITTEN HISTORY OF THE GREAT INSURRECTION

The sack of Neptune didn't happen after Prometheus arrived, though the first conversation between him and Dominik de Febian went down in history as if it had.

The war for Neptune came next, a bloody, costly war I'll write about at a later time. There's a lot to say about everything that happened from Phoenix to his arrival. Some of it is understood, while we just guess at the rest. I won't skip on that in this history, but for right now, I want to talk a bit about the man instead of the circumstances.

The AllMother called Prometheus the truth and the way as if he were an ancient god who was worshipped before the Commonwealth existed. Prometheus is no god, but that doesn't mean the AllMother was wrong.

The truth is his will.

The way is his compass, always moving us toward the end goal.

What I know is this:

I planned a war down to the most minuscule details like the timing of ship landings and line movements. I sent men to retrieve our brother as Prometheus had done for me. I performed at the very top of my abilities, both in planning and fighting.

I lost it all, everything we'd built, and from what Jeeves said about the atmosphere, probably my life as well. I'd lost the war in the first few hours, a war that had taken a thousand years to even happen.

Me. I did that.

Then Prometheus arrived, and with a well-targeted strike against a deadly enemy, changed everything.

This war is here in earnest now. There's no going back. There's nowhere to go back *to*. Our home will be in this Solar System, or we're going to die.

It's that simple.

I have faith. His truth and his way will get us to Earth, and from there, may the gods show us favor.

AUTHOR NOTES - DAVID BEERS
WRITTEN NOVEMBER 30, 2021

The final arc is upon us.

In fact, there are only two books left.

I don't know if it was necessary to leave Alistair out of Book Seven for such large chunks; perhaps, it could've been a more compelling book to have him in the midst, fighting. I don't write to make a compelling book, however, but to make a compelling story. Alistair's story is one of nine books, and for this to end the way I wanted, he had to learn something.

It's something that I've had to learn over and over: I'm only in control of my actions, but nothing of this universe around me. It's a hard lesson, especially for a control freak like me, but luckily I never had to fly into a fucking black hole to learn it.

Writing is a different exercise for different people. It holds different meanings, different purposes. For me, it's an expression of the soul – I just try to have some badass fight scenes while expressing myself.

Also, regarding Book Six's author notes: Mike was definitely early, and thus he missed mine, as *mine* are always right on time. Just like Alistair. ;)

I wonder what his excuse will be this time? I bet he blames it on Steve, though, in that case, he'd probably be right.

I kid, I kid. It was probably my fault, just don't tell either of them. I'll never live it down.

All the best,
db

Thank you for not only reading this story but these author notes as well.

I cannnnNOT believe David Beers just threw down the "I'm always on time" gauntlet! That is so far from the truth that Truth itself just cringed.

No, really!

Unfortunately, in good faith, I can't discuss any of the times David "allegedly" was late. In fact, I have to go so far as to say I might...or might not...be under NDA to never speak of those situations.

So, I'll talk about a different story with David involved.

Picture the scene... The time was about...two years ago before Covid. Four guys were sitting around a table at Jessie Rae's BBQ in Las Vegas.

It's Craig Martelle (massive sci-fi and thriller author and great friend), Mike Bray (owner of Wolfpack Publishing and another friend), David Beers, and me.

When you get four guys telling stories about their past, it is commonly known by the euphemism "bullshitting." I threw Mike Bray under the bus by admitting that his stories always seem to have him end up in jail.

For example.

There was this one time in college when Mike got busted for a small fight after a rodeo and was thrown in the drunk tank in New Mexico. There was that other time he was in a fight during his best friend's wedding dinner (the best friend started it), and another time when he was drunk during a stag party and was driving golf balls down the motel/hotel's hallway late one night.

I barely touched on the stories about Mike and the police.

David, laughing his ass off at all of these as Mike confirms the truth, glances at Craig and asks him if he was ever tossed into jail.

Craig, a former Marine who worked in areas tangential to spying while in the military, looks up and says, "No, but I was tossed out of and banned from a country."

That was when I learned you can trump a lifetime of stories where you get tossed into the slammer overnight by getting tossed out of Russia for something you didn't do.

For asking that question, I'll raise a root beer in David's direction and say, "Salut!"

Have a good week, or weekend. Talk to you in the next story!

Ad Aeternitatem,

Michael Anderle

Nemesis

She's coming and no one can stop her...

An alien Queen, Morena, was removed from power and forced into exile. Doomed to roam space forever, with no hope of return.

Until a random party brings a man named Michael to her crashed ship. For the first time in millennia, Morena sees her salvation. First, in Michael ... and then Earth. The perfect place to repopulate her species. And those already here? **They can bow or die.**

As Morena begins her conquest, can Michael warn the world before it's too late? Can anyone stop the most powerful force the world has ever seen?

Earth's final Nemesis has arrived.

Don't miss this pulse-pounding science fiction series! If you love thought provoking thrill-rides, grab this book today!

The Singularity

One thousand years in the future, humans no longer rule...

In the early twenty-first century, humanity marveled at its greatest creation: Artificial Intelligence. They never foresaw the consequences of such a creation, though...

Now, in a world where humans must meet specifications to continue living, a man named Caesar emerges. Different, both in thought and talent, Caesar somehow slipped through the genetic net meant to catch those like him.

Eyes are falling on Caesar now, though, and he can no longer hide. The Artificial Intelligence wants him dead, but others want him to lead their revolution...

Can one man stand against humanity's greatest creation? A don't-miss epic science fiction novel that pits one man fighting for the future of all people!

Red Rain

What would you do if you couldn't stop killing?

John Hilt lives The American Dream. His corner office looks out on Dallas's beautiful skyline. His amazing wife and children love him. His father and sister adore him. John has it all.

Except every few years, when Harry shows back up. Harry wants John to kill people. Harry wants to watch the world burn.

Murderous thoughts take hold of John, and as flames ignite across his life, the sky doesn't send cool rain water, but blood to feed their hunger.

If you love taut, psychological thrillers, grab Red Rain today and prepare to sleep with the lights on!

The Devil's Dream

He'll raise the dead, at all costs...

Perhaps the smartest man to ever live, Matthew Brand changed the world by twenty-five years old. In his mid-thirties, he still shaped the world as he wanted, until cops gunned down his son on the street.

Brand's life changed then. He forgot about bettering Earth and started trying to resurrect his son.

Eventually, Brand's mind overpowered even death's mysteries; he discovered how to bring back the dead--he only needed living bodies to make his son's life possible again. Why not use the bodies of those who killed his son? In the largest manhunt the FBI's ever experienced, how do they stop a man who can calculate all the odds and stack them in his favor?

https://www.instagram.com/lmbpn_publishing/

https://www.bookbub.com/authors/michael-anderle